The Wish Stealers

BY TRACY TRIVAS

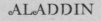

ALADDIN

New York   London   Toronto   Sydney

ALADDIN

An imprint of Simon & Schuster Children's Publishing Division
1230 Avenue of the Americas, New York, NY 10020
First Aladdin paperback edition February 2011
Copyright © 2010 by Tracy Trivas
All rights reserved, including the right of reproduction in whole or in part in any form.
ALADDIN is a trademark of Simon & Schuster, Inc., and related logo is a registered trademark of Simon & Schuster, Inc.
Also available in an Aladdin hardcover edition.
For information about special discounts for bulk purchases, please contact Simon & Schuster Special Sales at 1-866-506-1949 or business@simonandschuster.com.
The Simon & Schuster Speakers Bureau can bring authors to your live event. For more information or to book an event contact the Simon & Schuster Speakers Bureau at 1-866-248-3049 or visit our website at www.simonspeakers.com.
Designed by Lisa Vega
The text of this book was set in Adobe Garamond.
Manufactured in the United States of America 0111 OFF
2 4 6 8 10 9 7 5 3 1
The Library of Congress has cataloged the hardcover edition as follows:
Trivas, Tracy.
The wish stealers / by Tracy Trivas. — 1st Aladdin hardcover ed.
p. cm.
Summary: Sixth-grader Griffin Penshine has always believed wishes can come true, and so when a strange woman curses her with a box of pennies, Griffin fears her evil desires will come true until she returns each penny to the person who first wished upon it.
ISBN 978-1-4169-8725-3 (hc)
[1. Wishes—Fiction. 2. Coins—Fiction. 3. Blessing and cursing—Fiction.
4. Supernatural—Fiction. 5. Schools—Fiction. 6. Family life—Kansas—Fiction.
7. Kansas—Fiction.] I. Title.
PZ7.T7376Wis 2010
[Fic]—dc22
2009042742
ISBN 978-1-4169-8726-0 (pbk)
ISBN 978-1-4169-9733-7 (eBook)

For Alexander and Hadley,
my Wish Givers

Chapter

1

Griffin Penshine had three freckles under her left eye that sometimes looked like stars. This was a good thing, as Griffin was always wishing. She wished when a ladybug landed on a windowsill, she wished on dandelion dust, and she even wished on tumbling eyelashes. In fact, she often rescued the eyelash of a friend and reminded her to wish. But then again, Griffin always noticed the smallest of details. She could track her way out of a forest, spotted everything from worms to woodbeetles, and giggled at absurd words on menus like "jumbo shrimp." Griffin also liked certain things a certain way. She loved peanut butter on brownies, hated wearing turtlenecks, and insisted her mom buy cool mint toothpaste.

On the last Sunday of a hot Kansas summer, a ladybug flew in through Griffin's bedroom window and landed on her arm. Griffin smiled and opened her new blue-lined notebook and scribbled her next few wishes.

I wish all vegetables had cool names like bok choy, alfalfa, and parsnip.

I wish to become an amazing bass guitarist.

Griffin thought for a moment and then crossed off her first wish. She didn't want to waste a wish on vegetables. As for being a great bass guitarist, she wished for that every chance she got. Too bad she hadn't wished for protection.

"Griffin!" called her mom from downstairs. "We're going to be late." Griffin's mother, an astronomer, loved to calculate the time it would take to reach Saturn, Neptune, the Andromeda galaxy, and even the center of town. She knew if they didn't leave in five minutes they would not make their afternoon appointments. Dr. Penshine hated being late, and she loved to wear her huge collection of inspirational T-shirts that said things like SAVE THE EARTH. Only now that

Dr. Penshine was pregnant, the words stretched over her huge bump and read SAVE THE EAR.

Griffin giggled from the top of the stairs. "I like your shirt, Mom."

Dr. Penshine looked down at her bulging tummy. "Ears need saving too!" she said, laughing.

Griffin grabbed her bass guitar. Her long, beautiful, shiny red hair swung in the sunlight as she ran down the stairs and slid into the car.

"Before I drop you off at your music lesson, I need to make a fifteen-minute stop at Mr. Schmidt's shop," said her mom. "He received a shipment of artifacts from Egypt—ancient clay scarab beetles—and an antique model of the solar system from an English castle. He's saving them for me."

"Okay," said Griffin. She didn't mind stopping. Mr. Schmidt, their neighbor, had the strangest objects at his store. Maybe she would find something for her pet turtle, Charlemagne's, terrarium or a good luck charm for tomorrow—the first day of sixth grade at her new middle school—or some cool object for her Mysterium Collection Box that she hid under her bed.

Although it was only a shoe box with a rectangle of midnight blue felt lining the bottom, inside the box were two eagle feathers passed down by her great-grandfather before they became illegal to keep, half of a heart from her best-friend-forever necklace she shared with Libby Barrett, an old lace valentine her grandma Penshine had made as a girl, and three smooth stones.

Her grandma had given her the three lucky stones: a moonstone thought to have the power to grant wishes, a tigereye for courage, and a piece of purple amethyst. Her grandma said Leonardo da Vinci believed amethyst could protect people from evil and make them smarter.

Too bad she didn't take her purple stone in her pocket that morning. But she wouldn't think of that until it was too late.

A COLLECTIBLES, ANTIQUES, AND WONDERS sign hung above the door to Mr. Schmidt's tiny shop.

Griffin pushed open the door. Rusted bells jingled, and smells of dust, must, and exotic spices twisted up her nose. Long rows of glass shelves with faded lace fans, heavy silver hand mirrors, ladies' hair combs made of bone and shell, and stained decks of old maid cards glowed under the dim cabinet light.

At the back of the store, from behind a velvet curtain, Mr. Schmidt poked his head out. "Good morning, Dr. Penshine and Griffin," he said. "Let me get that prized antique I was telling you about." He shuffled away.

Griffin bent her head over a glass case, looking at the lapis eye of a peacock feather and a mirror made of pitch-black polished stone. A handwritten card attached to the exotic feather read: *From India 1913. Believed to make wishes come true.* Under the circular black stone the card read: *Obsidian mirror—used by the ancient Alchemists, passed down from Aztec priests. See your future!*

A chill blasted through the room, and Griffin looked up. Behind the counter appeared the oldest woman she had ever seen, wearing a long black dress with a wilting red lily pinned to it. With her greasy gray hair pulled tightly into a bun, the woman's face resembled a shriveled apple. Wicked wrinkles gouged in her skin, and a grid of purple veins looked like a grotesque spiderweb covering her face.

Griffin stared.

The woman's eyes drank in Griffin. Then in a low, crackly voice she said, "Only once before in my life have I seen that shiny liquid red color woven into a girl's hair—half autumn leaves and caramel kisses, half blazing sunset."

"Griff?" said her mom, coming from behind her. "Find anything?"

"Dr. Penshine and Griffin, forgive me," said Mr. Schmidt,

returning from the back room. "I need to introduce my great-aunt Mariah Weatherby Schmidt, who has come from Topeka to visit for a few weeks. She offered to help me today at the store."

A sinister smile curled on Mariah's cracked lips. "What a pleasure to meet you, Griffin Penshine. What are you looking for today?"

"Something for my turtle's terrarium or something lucky for the first day of school," Griffin said.

"I see," said Mariah, her yellow eyes narrowing. "I have just the thing for you. One moment."

Griffin looked at her mom, but she was too busy examining the antique model of the solar system.

Mariah disappeared through the heavy curtain. Griffin's head spun. The scent of spices, mandarin orange, dried lavender, cloves, and incense pounded in her brain. "Mom, I have a headache. I'm going to wait outside."

"Okay. I'll be five more minutes," she said.

Just as Griffin's hand touched the doorknob to leave, Mariah's cold hand brushed hers. "Where are you going, dear?" She held out a ring box. "This is for you."

"What is it?" asked Griffin, not moving from the door.

"Open it," the old woman said, beckoning with her long, spindly fingers.

Griffin slowly took the box from Mariah's bony hand and looked inside. Beams of light shot out all over the ceiling like lasers, illuminating the store. Carefully Griffin removed a single Indian Head penny.

It bounced in her hand.

"That's the shiniest penny I've ever seen," said Dr. Penshine.

"I'm sure it is," said Mariah. "I never forget to . . . polish it. It is priceless. An Indian Head penny from 1897. Very rare, very valuable, and shall we say . . . very lucky."

"Wow," said Griffin, mesmerized by the pulsing glow. Droplets of light sprinkled all over the room.

"It must be yours!" said Mariah, her eyes flashing.

The strangest sensation knotted inside Griffin, part repulsion, part desire. "How much is it?" she asked.

"It is my special gift to you." Mariah smiled wickedly. For a moment Griffin swore Mariah looked younger, luminescent, something wild and alive in her eyes.

"I can't take something priceless for free," said Griffin, now blinded by the magnificent penny.

"Just promise you'll keep it shiny, and it will be . . . worth it to me. You will accept my gift, won't you?"

Every cell in Griffin's body fought to say, "No. No, thank you!" But the Indian Head penny shined so hypnotically that Griffin could hardly speak. Her pupils dilated from the beams shooting off the penny. She tried to shake her head, stop the odd breeze that whirled around her body. *No,* she mouthed, but no sound came out. Instead "Yes" exhaled from her lips.

Mariah froze. Then very deliberately she said, "It is done. Let me get a box of polishing cloths from the back for you. Give me a few moments to find it."

Griffin tucked the penny into her pocket, and it burned against her skin.

✳ ✳ ✳

Penny, penny bring me luck,
'cause I'm the one who picked you up.

Chapter

2

How neat to have a lucky penny for the first
day of school, Griff," said her mom, carrying
her own prized antique back to their car.

"Yeah, but why do you think Mariah said 'It is done'?"
asked Griffin. Goose bumps sprouted on her arms when she
repeated the words.

"Probably just an old-fashioned saying. She *really* is
ancient," said her mom.

Suddenly a cloud above them smothered the light in the
sky. Both Griffin and her mom looked up and at the exact
same time said, "It looks like it's going to rain!"

"WISH!" Griffin said, smiling. She believed that

whenever two people said the exact same thing at the exact same time, a wish would be granted. Griffin counted quickly on her fingers. "It looks like it's going to rain" had seven words in it. "Seven wishes!" she said to her mom.

"You already know what I wish for seven times," said Dr. Penshine with a dreamy smile on her face. Griffin knew she wished for a healthy baby. Griffin climbed into the car as raindrops started falling in giant plops. Her mom carefully set the antique in the backseat.

Griffin looked at the darkening sky outside the car window. Silently she thought of her wishes . . .

I wish to become an amazing bass guitarist.

Griffin had been studying bass for the last four years with her guitar teacher, Mr. Castanara.

I wish my new school smells like warm chocolate chip cookies!

She smiled. Her old school smelled like erasers, floor cleaner, and sharpened number two pencils. Maybe her new school would be different.

I wish for a baby sister.

She loved the girl names Janis, D'Arcy, and Michelle, after her favorite female rock stars.

I wish for Grandma Penshine to get well soon.

For the last year her grandma had been having unexplainable dizzy spells and horrible headaches.

I wish the dentist will not have to pull my two back molars for braces.

I wish no kid in the world has nasty green food caught in his teeth and no one tells him.

I wish when it stops raining that no soggy worms will fry on the sidewalk the next sunny day.

Just as she made her last wish, the sky turned a greenish hue, the air hung still and deadly, and heavy moisture weighed upon her skin. Suddenly thunder roared and needles of rain unleashed from the sky.

"Summer storm!" said her mom, starting the engine.

Thunder clapped as javelins of lightning flew through the sky and bounded over the rooftops. Rain, wind, and leaves swooshed violently all around the car.

"This is unbelievable!" said her mom, fiddling with the

radio. "It's like a warm and cold air mass just collided in front of us."

"Attention, Dadesville citizens. This is from the National Weather Service." A series of high-pitched beeps blasted through the speakers. "A tornado warning has been issued for Dadesville. Please take immediate shelter in your basements. A tornado is headed directly toward Dadesville."

Tornado sirens posted on poles throughout town suddenly screeched out a steady alarm, which vibrated the car's windows.

"We've got five minutes to get home!" said her mom, swerving the car around in a fierce crazy eight.

Griffin shuddered. An ominous emerald sky now cloaked the town. When a tornado circled its prey, the sky turned green. Outside the car window, the wind raged.

"Hang on, Griff!" said her mom, speeding the car through the street toward their home. Trees swayed like toothpicks, and the roofs of houses cringed from the heavy rain attacking them.

Finally they made it to their garage. Dr. Penshine took a deep breath and rubbed her big belly. "I'm going to go get our portable radio and a flashlight. Run down to the basement and wait for me. I'll call Dad on my cell phone and see how far away he is from home."

Griffin ran through the door. With her bass guitar swinging on her shoulder, she grabbed Charlemagne from his kitchen terrarium and leapt down a flight of creaky stairs to their basement. The single lightbulb hanging from the ceiling hardly lit up the dank room. Her family never used their basement except to store potatoes, onions, and sports equipment. Griffin shivered and sat on the cold cement floor. She realized she was still clutching in her left hand the small box of polishing cloths Mariah had given her.

"Dad is stuck at Grandma's house," called her mom from the top of the stairs. "He can't drive home now. He's going to stay in Grandma's basement with her. I need to grab some blankets for cover."

"Can I help?" called Griffin.

"No! Stay downstairs! The tornado is moving closer!" yelled her mom.

The penny that Mariah had given her felt hot in her pocket.

Does copper attract heat? Griffin wondered. She hoped her best friend, Libby, was safe in her basement with her family. She tried to call to see if she was okay, but her cell phone was dead.

"Mom, can I run upstairs and use the kitchen phone to call Libby?" Griffin yelled.

"No! Stay off the phone! With all this lightning, that's how you get electrocuted!"

Right when her mom said the word "electrocuted," thunder crashed so deafeningly that the entire house shook, and the clasp on the box of polishing cloths sprang open. A few soft cotton rags toppled out. Griffin scooped up the cloths, and a burst of light exploded out of the box. A massive glow lit up her face. Concealed beneath the polishing cloths rested ten radiant pennies in a thick black velvet pad. One slot was empty. "WOW!" gasped Griffin.

After pulling the penny from her pocket, Griffin placed it in the unfilled slot. It fit perfectly. A box of eleven perfect pennies! Gently she pulled the first penny out of its slot. Attached to it was a narrow faded yellow label stuck across the width of the coin. One word was written on the label with a black pen. In the most precise handwriting, the letters spelled "puppy."

She pulled out the next penny. The narrow label attached to it read "no homework." The next one read "STOP" in all uppercase letters. Another one read in tiny, tiny letters "change the world." The next penny: "popular."

Griffin pulled out the second row of pennies. This one read "a baby." The next read "a dad," another one "success."

Another one read "most beautiful." Griffin held the dullest penny. It read "world peace."

"Huh?" said Griffin aloud.

Are these people's wishes? she thought. A powerful thunder blast pounded the sky and jolted her house to its foundation.

Copper light zigzagged on the ceiling from the pennies' glow. Griffin slipped her fingers around the inside edge of the box and discovered the slotted velvet lining was loose. Peeling back the velvet, she felt the bottom of the box and found an old, yellowed envelope. Across the front, in that same strange handwriting, it read:

To: Griffin Penshine, the girl who accepted my "lucky penny"

From: Mariah Weatherby Schmidt

When I saw you, a memory sprang into my head. Only once before in my life have I seen hair the color red like yours, like a gussied-up copper penny. I am very, very old. Some people might call me ancient. Right, my dear? But the curse must live on. All that work for nothing would be such a waste. You are the one. Inside the envelope is my story.

A horrible feeling tossed in Griffin's stomach. Gingerly she opened the envelope and spread the fragile typed letter on the floor.

Long ago, when I was hardly done being a girl, I accepted my first job as a secretary at an inn. The inn stood at the crossroads of Topeka, Kansas, and a bubbling fountain graced the center courtyard.

The first time it happened, it was an accident. On a hot Kansas day I heard a plunk-splash in the water. I pushed away the white lace curtain to see a little boy and his mom standing before the fountain. The boy said, "I wish for a boat." From high up in my office I saw exactly where his penny landed. That's how it began.

At night, after working late, I would dip my hand into the fountain, scoop up the wet pennies, and toss people's wishes around in my palm. A person's penny could be a wish for a pony, but it bought me a pretty silk ribbon instead. For years I swept up the change, buying myself sweets, eating people's wishes. I loved to twist their dreams in my hair with the fancy ribbons I bought for myself. I heard a lot of wishes in those years, as people stood alone before the fountain, not thinking.

I could hear the plunks and pings of the coins diving through the water. And the things they wished for! Silly things, sad things, important things.

Sometimes people were really desperate and would throw dimes into the fountain. Dimes could buy you something really nice back then. Dimes didn't plunk in the water like a penny. A dime was like a little ping. Ping. Ping. Like a silver raindrop. It was a beautiful sound. I'd wait a few minutes till the people were inside fiddling with their bags and I'd rush out, pretend I was cooling my fingers, trailing them in the water. But when I pulled my hand out, a wish was captured in my palm.

✳ ✳ ✳

I am 92 years old. After all these years, these eleven pennies never lost their glow. Sometimes they even felt hot in my hand. They are all Indian Head pennies, much more potent and valuable than regular pennies. I saw exactly where they landed, heard the secret wishes aloud. I labeled them so I wouldn't forget. I never felt a drop of guilt either. Like my father told me when I was a young girl, I wasn't going to amount to much so I should just stop dreaming and wishing and filling my head with silly thoughts.

You are the new guardian of the eleven stolen wishes. You are the new Wish Stealer.

There are three rules to wish stealing:

1) A Wish Stealer's good wishes will not come true.

2) A Wish Stealer's evil wishes will come true.

3) If a Wish Stealer tells anyone about the

curse, he or she will be cursed for life, and the person he or she tells will never have any of his or her wishes come true.

P.S. Once you've accepted the wishes, they are yours. IT IS DONE. You can't dump them into the garbage, or toss the whole box into a fountain and forget about them.

In that same strange handwriting as on the envelope, she had written in pen at the bottom:

P.P.S. You could trick someone into accepting the box, but you don't seem like that kind of girl—yet. The penny I gave you at the shop flew like a leaping ballerina vaulting into the water. That person didn't say her wish out loud, but her penny was as dazzling as her long red hair.

Griffin stood in shock. *A Wish Stealer.* She pulled a penny from its slot. "STOP" was written on its label. *Stop what?* she wondered. Her head pounded. Mariah Weatherby Schmidt had tricked her! Furiously she stuffed the box of pennies into the side pocket of her guitar case, and clenched Mariah's letter in her hands.

Griffin's mom clunked into the basement. "The tornado is getting closer. Are you okay?"

"I . . . ," said Griffin, staring at her mom and her big belly.

"Griff, what's in your hand?"

Mariah's letter flopped like a limp fish in her palm. "Uhh, a letter I was writing to . . ." She gulped. "Grandma." Just as she said the word "grandma," a bolt of lightning struck the house.

✳   ✳   ✳

Penny for your thoughts,
nickel for your dreams.

Chapter

The next morning rain dribbled outside the Penshines' kitchen. Dr. Penshine set three hot blueberry pancakes on Griffin's plate and three on Griffin's dad's plate. "Pancakes to celebrate the first day of school," said Dr. Penshine.

"You can say that again!" said Griffin's dad, reading the morning paper before heading to Eastern Kansas University, where he taught law. "It says here that Dadesville hasn't experienced such erratic weather in the last hundred years. One minute it's a summer day; the next minute a tornado nearly destroys the town."

"I can't believe our house was struck by lightning! Thank goodness you weren't near water or on the phone, Griff!" said Dr. Penshine.

Griffin chewed the mountain of pancakes and nodded with her mouth full. Last night, when the announcer on the portable radio had said the tornado had diverted its course and she was allowed upstairs, she hid the box of pennies under her bed. Would none of her good wishes come true? Could she really ruin other people's wishes if she told them about the pennies? she wondered. She knew her dad wished for wars to end and to get tenure. Griffin shook her head. She believed in wishes, but not in Wish Stealers. Mariah had to be totally bonkers, a senile old lady, *ancient*, like her mom had said. Griffin refused to believe in curses. There was no way a box of Indian Head pennies could hurt her.

She decided to just enjoy her mom's blueberry pancakes.

"Griff, I forgot to tell you. When you were upstairs getting dressed, the dentist called. It turns out that she is going to have to pull your back molars for braces. There's an opening next week."

The pancakes morphed into a lumpy ball in her throat. Wasn't that one of her wishes? *I wish the dentist will not have to pull my two back molars for braces.*

If you are a Wish Stealer, none of your good wishes will come true blasted through her head.

Probably just a coincidence, Griffin reassured herself, but she lost her appetite anyway.

✳ ✳ ✳

Coincidence . . . or . . .
COIN-incidence?

Chapter

4

Griffin slid into the car. Charlemagne had acted strangely all morning, afraid to come out of his shell. Griffin thought it had to be the weather. She refused to think about Mariah or the curse. After all, it was the first day of school. She and her best friend, Libby, had planned their outfits a week before and had promised to wear their gold heart best-friends-forever necklaces today.

She wore her new canvas Converse sneakers that she'd spent all summer decorating with permanent colored pens. One side of each sneaker was blue, and the other side sported purple paisleys. "Go Green" was written on the white rubber rim. A peace sign swirled on the tops. She'd even sat on her bedroom floor coloring her shoelaces in tiny multicolored stripes. That had left little marks like an outlined centipede on her hardwood floor that she thought looked supercool (a feeling her mom didn't share).

Dr. Penshine parked the car in front of Griffin's new school and read, "George Washington LeGrange Middle School. You're growing up so fast, Griff." Her mom's eyes moistened.

"I love you, Mom," said Griffin, hugging her. Lately her mom cried over Hallmark card commercials, a dead goldfish, and every time someone mentioned that the planet Pluto had gotten demoted.

"Pregnancy hormones," explained Griffin's dad each week. He also stocked the freezer with Häagen-Dazs mint chip and butter pecan ice cream for Dr. Penshine's cravings, which made Griffin love it even more that her mom was pregnant.

"Have a great day!" called her mom.

Griffin dashed toward the school lobby, where she planned to meet Libby. Giddy in her raincoat, with her hood flying off, she splashed through the puddles, forgetting all about stolen wishes. Looking up at the rain, she hoped each and every drop would either turn to chocolate or grant a year of good luck for the person it fell on.

Griffin did not notice Mariah across the street, drenched in her long black raincoat, staring at her like a waiting crow. An evil smile curled on Mariah's cracked lips. Through the cold, misty rain Mariah crept closer to the school.

✳   ✳   ✳

Beware the person with
the Buddha smile and snake's heart.
—Chinese proverb

Chapter
5

Mariah pounced across the flooding street. Her shoes slapped over the sidewalk, and her cold palm pushed open the school doors. Inside the school lobby she smoothed her hair and opened her black bag. After pulling out a delicate flowered scarf, she tied it over her hair, removed her black coat, and pinned a bright red flower, a lily, the same color as Griffin's hair, onto her dress. Mariah chanted under her breath, "Stars, hide your fires. Let not light see my black and deep desires." She cackled in the hallway and slithered toward the front office.

Locker doors slammed, and the buzz of students swarmed

through the polished halls. So many kids jammed the corridors that it was hard to walk and not get smacked by a giant backpack or an oncoming slew of kids. Griffin and Libby tried to push their way toward room 13, first period English class. Middle school was nothing like fifth grade, where students stayed in one classroom.

"Come on, Libbs," said Griffin.

"I'm trying!" said Libby when some towering eighth graders cut in front of her.

Libby had a cute upturned nose, warm brown eyes, and shoulder-length blond curls that bobbed as she walked. Today she wore a superbright pink, yellow, and green striped sweater that looked like it spent its free time keeping ships from crashing into the shore.

"Room 13, " said Griffin, reading her schedule and leading Libby toward the opposite side of the school building. Libby had no sense of direction, loved garlic mashed potatoes, and dreamed of being a famous artist like Frida Kahlo one day. She loved to tape pictures from magazines all over her bedroom wall and make origami out of silver bubble gum wrappers. Most of all she loved hanging around Griffin's grandma, who was a painter and gave them lessons on the weekends when she felt well enough.

Griffin, on the other hand, wanted to be a rocket scientist or a rock star. She was also very proud of her sneakers. They entered the classroom and grabbed two desks toward the front. Both of their BFF heart necklaces glowed from the raindrops that had fallen on them.

Just as Griffin sat in the seat, "Griffin Penshine, Griffin Penshine, please come downstairs to the front office" blasted over the loudspeaker.

"Huh?" said Griffin. "That's weird. Did I forget something? Be right back. Can you save my seat?" For a moment a strange feeling crept over Griffin. *Could this have anything to do with Mariah?* she thought. But she shook her head and told herself she was being silly.

"Sure," said Libby.

Griffin powered through the emptying halls to the front office.

The strong scent of lilies wafted through the stairwell. Like cloying perfume or a dying bouquet in a funeral home, the smell shot up Griffin's nose and gave her a headache. Griffin walked into the office.

Sitting behind the administrator's desk stacked with unopened mail, a jolly woman with a ruddy face and a booming voice said, "You must be Griffin Penshine."

"Yes," said Griffin.

"I'm Mrs. Davis, and you have the nicest, sweetest grandma in the whole world," she said.

"How do you know?" Griffin asked.

"She just came in from that nasty rain to give you something she forgot—a first-day-of-school gift! Said she'd been waiting *years* to give it to you. Isn't that so sweet?" said Mrs. Davis, leaning her weight over her desk and handing a small box to Griffin.

Griffin beamed. Even in this terrible weather, with her grandma not feeling well, she'd still taken the time to drive to school. She adored her grandma Penshine. Dropping off a special gift for her was just like something her grandmother would do. While Griffin's mom used to write notes with a nontoxic black pen on a banana like *I'm bananas over you!* and stick it in her lunch bag, her grandma gave magical gifts like a hand-knit bag with lucky stones and a four leaf clover inside. (Charlemagne ate the clover by accident, but Grandma Penshine said not to worry, it just made Charlemagne a very lucky turtle.) Griffin opened the box. A tiny golden key lay inside with a note: *Good luck. From Mariah.*

All the color drained from Griffin's face.

❋   ❋   ❋

Good luck or bad luck can flip on a dime . . . or a penny.

Chapter

6

Dashing back to first period English class, Griffin couldn't stop sneezing. The smell of dying lilies barreled through the hall. *Mariah pretended to be my grandma!* The thought enraged her. *What is this key for?* She sneezed five more times.

Griffin clenched the key in her hand and darted into a bathroom. She stuffed her pocket with toilet paper for her runny nose. Finally she made it back to room 13. She quietly opened the door and scanned the sea of heads for Libby's blond hair and striped sweater. But the seat next to Libby, the one she'd asked her to save, was taken. A beautiful girl with long brown hair as silky as mink, and with the high preppie collar of her shirt turned up, sat there. Griffin walked to the one empty desk in the back corner of the classroom.

That smell. She couldn't get that sickly sweet smell out of her nose. "Haaaaachuuuuuuu! Haaaachuuu! Haaa-chuuuuuuu!" Griffin sneezed uncontrollably.

"Ewww," said a boy in front of her.

"Excuse me," said Griffin.

"Gesundheit!" said the teacher.

Libby turned around and mouthed *I'm sorry* and tipped her head toward the girl who'd taken Griffin's seat.

Rain hit the classroom windows, and the sky darkened.

"Whoa! Look at the sky!" a boy exclaimed.

"Creepy!" said a girl.

"'By the clock 'tis day / And yet dark night strangles the travelling lamp,'" quoted Mrs. Gideon, the English teacher. She had short silver-gray hair and wore a long skirt and a necklace made from chunky, colorfully glazed pottery pieces. "What perfect weather to begin our study of Shakespeare's condensed *Macbeth*!" Mrs. Gideon clapped her hands together. "Some people think this play is a bit advanced for sixth graders, but I say nonsense. It's about desires, greedy rulers, and betrayal—themes found in most of your computer games."

On the board Mrs. Gideon wrote, *Lilies that fester smell far worse than weeds*, and drew a witch's hat next to the sentence. "Everyone has three minutes to write down on a piece of paper what they think this quote means."

Is this why the school smells so bad? Griffin wondered. *Was it part of the lesson?* Griffin stared at her paper. Suddenly her hand felt possessed and she scrawled out a sentence.

"Okay, class. Time's up! Pass up your papers so I can read some aloud," said Mrs. Gideon. She flipped through some of the answers and stopped on one paper. "Who is David Hunt?" called the teacher.

David raised his hand.

"You wrote 'This quote means weeds really stink, but beautiful flowers stink worse,'" read Mrs. Gideon. "Interesting." She rustled through more papers. "Who is Griffin Penshine?"

Griffin raised her hand.

Mrs. Gideon smiled and read Griffin's paper, "'This quote is really about people. Some bad people are like weeds, ugly on the inside and outside. But what's worse is to be a good person who turns bad, does cruel things, and rots on the inside.'"

"Very good. Very good, Griffin," said Mrs. Gideon. "Maybe you'll be my new English star this year."

Griffin blushed. Libby turned around and smiled at her. The gorgeous girl next to Libby swiveled her head at Griffin. She narrowed her swampy green eyes. Griffin stared back. She had never seen eyes like that, green cold slits like a reptile's.

Just then the intercom blasted through the school. "Attention, students. This is your school principal, Dr. Yeldah. Please walk to the auditorium with your class for our welcome assembly."

All the kids packed up their bags. Griffin slid the tiny gold key in a side pocket of her backpack. *What awful thing does it open?* she thought, shivering.

Libby ran up to her. "Griff, I'm sorry. I told that girl I was saving that seat for you, but she just ignored me and sat there with her two friends."

"It's okay, Libby. It's not your fault. Maybe she got confused," she said.

"Why did you get called downstairs?" asked Libby.

Anger surged through Griffin. She couldn't believe Mariah had come to her new school!

"Griff?" said Libby.

"Uhh, my grandma"—Griffin gulped—"gave me a present."

"Students, stay in your group, line up on the far left of the auditorium, and file into the first three rows of seats," said Mrs. Gideon.

Libby and Griffin scanned the auditorium for some of

their friends from their old school and looked at all the new kids from different schools. Already they'd heard whispers about the cutest boy in sixth grade, Garrett Forester, whom they spotted on the opposite side of the auditorium.

While Griffin and Libby stood waiting to enter the row of seats, the girl who'd stolen Griffin's seat talked with her two friends. On her left stood a tall girl with long flat-ironed blond hair. She wore a necklace with the name Sasha sparkling in silver letters. On her right a girl with shoulder-length brown hair wore a pink headband with the name Martha embroidered on it in green. She wore a beige plaid designer skirt. Martha was saying, "Samantha, I just know you're going to win the Fresh Face! Prettiest New Face Contest. The whole school has already seen you model on your dad's infomercials. Everybody knows he's the best dermatologist with the *best* skin products in Kansas."

Samantha smiled, glad that Martha was talking so loudly. She turned around and looked Griffin and Libby up and down. "What school are you guys from?" she demanded.

"We went to Dadesville Elementary," said Libby.

"We went to Westminster *Private* School," said Samantha. Sasha and Martha did not move or smile.

"Isn't that the school with its own planetarium? My mom said the planetarium is really cool," said Griffin.

"It's totally lame. I hate planetariums," said Samantha. "Wait, is your mom the town astronomer, Dr. Penshine, the one who always wears those stupid T-shirts?"

Red flames shot up Griffin's face. Lilies. That horrible smell of putrefied lilies crept up her nostrils. She sneezed five times.

"Disgusting!" snarled Samantha. "Use a Kleenex! You almost ruined my cashmere sweater!"

Griffin reached into her pocket for a tissue and blew her nose loudly. "I *love* my mom's T-shirts," said Griffin. She did not notice that a long piece of toilet paper fell out of her pocket and onto the auditorium floor.

"Samantha Sloane," called the gym teacher. "Please go sit up on the stage. The principal chose your name out of a hat to welcome your class."

Samantha flipped her hair and walked away.

"I've seen her on her dad's infomercials. She's rich, beautiful, and mean—like a queen lizard," said Libby.

Somehow the image of a lizard queen walking around school cracked Griffin and Libby up, and they couldn't stop laughing.

Students finally settled into their seats. The principal walked onstage. "Welcome, students. Before I speak, I'd like to call up the three class representatives I randomly picked this morning to read our state motto in unison, 'To the Stars Through Difficulty! *Ad Astra Per Aspera*,' and tell me how he or she thinks this motto applies to our exciting school year!"

Samantha and the seventh- and eighth-grade representatives moved toward the microphone. Suddenly a group of boys roared with laughter. Griffin and Libby stared. The boys pointed at Samantha as she pranced in front of the whole school. A long piece of toilet paper was stuck to the heel of her designer shoe.

Samantha looked down, ripped the toilet paper off her shoe, and glared across the auditorium at Griffin.

✳ ✳ ✳

What a strange illusion it is
to suppose that beauty is goodness.
—Tolstoy

Chapter

Griffin's foot tapped under her desk in third period math class. A queasy feeling sloshed around inside her. Maybe she was just nervous; after all, it was the first day of school. But the stench of rotting lilies still coated the school from floor to ceiling, and she had already made an enemy.

"It reeks in this school!" kids cried in the hallways. Griffin spied a group of janitors searching for the source of the odor. "It's the oddest thing," she overheard one of them say. "We don't have a clue where this smell is coming from. We scoured the place from top to bottom only two days ago."

She thought back to her last seven wishes. Two had evaporated in the last 24 hours.

X   *I wish the dentist will not have to pull my two back molars for braces.*

X   *I wish my new school smells like warm chocolate chip cookies.*

She told herself she was being silly. It was all just coincidence. Wasn't it?

"Fifteen more minutes on these last math problems," said her teacher, Mrs. Sato. "Concentrate! I'm assessing your math skills from this quiz."

Was Griffin going crazy, imagining things? A tightness wrapped itself around her throat. She remembered her two most important wishes: *I wish for a baby sister. I wish for Grandma Penshine to get well soon.*

Chills, like sharpened fingernails, crept up her back. In case there was even the tiniest bit of bad luck stuck with Mariah's wishes, and these weren't coincidences, Griffin had to get rid of them.

"Griffin?" called Mrs. Sato.

"Yes?" she said.

"Are you okay?" the teacher asked, bending over her desk. "You've been very distracted ever since class began."

"I—I'm sorry, Mrs. Sato. I didn't get much sleep last night," said Griffin, gazing down at her paper. On it she had written her name, had numbered from one to eleven, and had drawn a large penny.

When Mrs. Sato walked away, Griffin wrote down Mariah Weatherby Schmidt's age, ninety-two, and the sentence from Mariah's letter—*hardly done being a girl*. What age would that be? Most people consider someone done being a girl or boy at eighteen, the official adult age. So if Mariah wrote that her first job was around this time, she was probably eighteen or a little younger. Griffin wrote $92 - 18 = 74$.

Seventy-four years ago, give or take a few years, Mariah Weatherby Schmidt had started stealing wish pennies from the fountain. All sorts of people of all ages made wishes. Griffin clasped her hand over her mouth. Griffin guessed a lot of the people whose wishes Mariah had stolen were probably dead!

Mrs. Burns leaned over Griffin's desk as she scribbled numbers fiercely on her notebook. "Much better, Griffin!"

Griffin smiled at her teacher, but her thoughts were flying. She was determined to make Mariah take back her box of stolen wishes after school.

✳   ✳   ✳

Refuse to take on other people's bad luck.

Chapter 8

L ate afternoon sunshine beat mercilessly down upon the asphalt. *It's as if the storm and rain never happened,* thought Griffin. She moved closer to Mr. Schmidt's house carrying Mariah's black box. Every drop of water had evaporated. On the sidewalk worms writhed, frying in the sun. Griffin grabbed a broken branch and tried to gently move worm after worm to the safety of the grass, but there were too many.

I wish when it stops raining that no soggy worms will fry on the sidewalk the next sunny day, ran through her head.

"This is awful," said Griffin. Crows circled above. "I wish . . . ," she began, but she stopped herself. For the first time in her life she had lost her confidence in wishing.

Up ahead of her was Mr. Schmidt's house. All the shades were drawn, and it looked sealed like a tomb. Griffin walked up to the front door and knocked three times. "Mr. Schmidt!" Griffin shouted, and knocked even harder. "Mr. Schmidt!"

"Griffin?" called a neighbor from next door.

"Hi, Mrs. Jasper," she answered.

"I heard all the commotion out here. I thought someone was knocking on my door," she said.

"I'm looking for Mr. Schmidt and his great-aunt. Do you know when they'll be back?" asked Griffin.

"Your family hasn't heard?"

Griffin shook her head.

"It happened around ten this morning," said Mrs. Jasper. "I'm sure it was pneumonia. The evening the tornado passed by I saw Mariah out on the front porch in the rain! Imagine sitting in a rocking chair in weather like that! I was about to call Mr. Schmidt to get his aunt out from that awful weather, I thought maybe she wasn't quite right in the head. She was very old, you know. Anyway, when I looked out again, she was gone. Mr. Schmidt said she lay down to take a nap this morning and died in her sleep. He said there was the strangest smile on her face. He's gone back to Topeka to arrange the funeral."

Griffin gasped.

"I know, dear," said Mrs. Jasper, coming closer to her. "These things can be very sad, but what a long life! Did you know his aunt?"

"Not really," she whispered.

"Nice lady, very old. Only been here a week. Imagine that," said Mrs. Jasper. "Mr. Schmidt asked me to get the mail. Was it something important you needed?"

"No, I . . . did his great-aunt have any children?"

"As far as I know she never married, and Mr. Schmidt was her only relative. But she wanted to be buried back in Topeka."

Griffin trudged home, now feeling the horrible heaviness of the box of stolen wishes in her hands.

* * *

The best way out is always through.
—Robert Frost

Chapter

S amantha's long hair swayed like a sheet of perfectly smooth silk. In English class the next day not one strand dared disobey her. She wore a designer dress with horseshoe logos all over it, bead bangle bracelets all up her right arm, leather riding boots, and a scarf knotted into a headband. Instead of a backpack she carried an Italian handbag her mom had handed down to her when she'd gotten bored with it. Some of the boys feared her, others had crushes on her, and the rest had a little bit of both. Girls chimed throughout the hall, "Hi, Samantha. You look amazing!" or "Oh, my gosh, Samantha. I *love* your dress!"

"What a wonderful start we had with *Macbeth*! A storm

to set our stage!" said Mrs. Gideon. "Now we will dive into the play, which opens with three witches telling Macbeth his fortune. Not what *will* happen, but what *could* happen as painted in the stars."

Griffin sat in the back row, stuck in that lonesome seat from the first day of class. Scanning the heads in front of her, she saw Samantha surrounded by new girls who wanted to be friends with her.

Her grandma always said, *To have a friend you must be a friend.* Griffin thought Samantha didn't seem like she'd be a kind friend, but it didn't seem to matter. Everything felt upside down, and Griffin hated not telling her parents, Libby, or any of her old friends at her lunch table about the way Mariah had tricked her. But what if something bad did happen, and everybody's wishes started unraveling if she told? She would never trick someone like Mariah had tricked her into accepting the box of wishes. If only there were a way to return the wishes. She sunk her head onto her folded hands and looked out the window at the shifting clouds.

"Macbeth and Banquo ask the witches to tell them their fortune," said Mrs. Gideon. She read from the play, "'If you can look into the seeds of time, / And say which grain will grow and which will not, Speak then to me . . .'

"It is only the second day of school, but I already have a surprise for you. The Shakespeare Is Not Dead Traveling Globe Theatre Company. They just arrived in town! Please welcome the three witches from *Macbeth*!" Mrs. Gideon clapped ecstatically.

From outside the hallway a wretched cackling echoed. Three stooped hags with straggly hair, dressed in black shredded rags, moth-bitten shawls, and pointy hats shuffled into the room.

Every student sat straight in his or her seat. Although everyone knew the witches were just actors, the women's faces looked wildly aged, bumpy with warts, and lined with a million creases. One of the witches carried a spell book under her arm, with the title *The Future, Fate & Mortal Wishes*.

"They look real!" whispered a student in front of Griffin. Chills ran up and down her spine. They did look real. Impossibly real. Horribly real.

"Double, double toil and trouble; / Fire burn, and cauldron bubble . . . Eye of newt and toe of frog, / Wool of bat and tongue of dog . . ." they crowed, hovering in a coven in front of the room. Griffin couldn't take her eyes off the spell book. *It's just a prop,* she reminded herself.

The three witches finished their lines and stood like

vultures, with their beady eyes scanning the classroom.

"Beyond lifelike!" said Mrs. Gideon. "Students, do you have any questions?"

Griffin's hand shot up. "What's in your spell book?"

The first witch answered, "Would you like to take a look, my dear?"

Griffin nodded, mesmerized by the witch's yellow eyes. Just like Mariah's.

The witch hobbled over to Griffin and dropped the spell book onto her desk. "Be quick, my dear. Time is almost up," she whispered.

Her face, so close to Griffin's own, looked familiar. Those pinched lips, sunken hollow cheeks, rotted skin, and dried desert of wrinkles . . .

"Next question for these otherworldly actors!" said Mrs. Gideon.

Griffin bent her head over the book and opened to the table of contents. Ancient mildew wafted up at her. She traced her finger down the page, feeling a covering of sticky cobwebs. *Chapter 4: Stealing and Returning Mortal Wishes.* Griffin turned to Chapter 4. Her heart raced as she read:

If one possesses a stolen wish, the best way to break its curse is to return the wish to

its rightful owner. That is the most powerful
magic. Be advised it takes some time for the
magic to work.

If that is impossible, one can return the
wish to a person who is on the same journey
as the original wisher. The magic is not as
strong, but if the intention is sincere, it may
work.

Griffin memorized each and every word. Then she read
the final sentence on the page.

If a stolen wish or wishes are not returned,
they corrupt the new owner, and all that is
good and full of light inside that person will
be destroyed. Evil will infest its host, and
tendrils of darkness soon will overtake him
or her.

Griffin's face lost all color.

"I'll be needing that back now, my dear. Did you find
it . . . *lucky*?" asked the witch, suddenly hovering over
Griffin.

"Uh, yes," said Griffin, looking deep into the witch's swirling eyes.

"Enchanted!" said Mrs. Gideon. "Let's give the three actors a huge round of applause."

Evil smiles set on the three crones' faces, their black teeth bared to all the students.

Bringgg rang the bell.

Libby waited for Griffin outside class. "Mrs. Gideon is really into this play!" said Libby, and she mimicked the teacher, "'Fair is foul, and foul is fair!' Those witches were freaky!"

"Yeah," said Griffin. Her head pounded.

Together they walked toward their bright orange lockers. Earlier that morning they had decorated them. Griffin had brought photos of her family, her grandma and her, Libby and Griffin river rafting on a giant inner tube, Charlemagne, a shooting star, Griffin jamming on her bass guitar, and Janis Joplin singing.

"Griff, look, is there something on your locker?" said Libby as they came closer.

Toilet paper streamed out from the locker vents, trailing all the way down to the floor.

"Samantha!" said Libby.

Griffin opened her locker. Toilet paper twisted inside like paper snakes. Just then Garrett Forester walked by. His dirty blond hair flopped over his bright blue eyes, and his jeans hung loose and baggy. "Whoa," he said, smiling at Griffin, who was now standing in a pool of toilet paper. "Cool photos," he added. "Is that you playing bass?"

"Yeah," she said.

"Awesome," he said, smiling again.

Griffin blushed as red as a fire engine.

✳ ✳ ✳

Genuine gold fears no fire.
—Chinese proverb

Chapter

10

Early the next morning Griffin opened the box of pennies and scooped up one for each pocket, and then tucked the box into her backpack. All night she had debated about what she should do. Mariah Weatherby Schmidt was dead. There was no returning the stolen wishes to her. Even if she gave the box back to Mr. Schmidt, he would probably stick it on a sagging shelf in his overstuffed garage or just dump it into the garbage. Then she might still be stuck with bad luck. She decided she would *try* to return some of the wishes to "a person who is on the same journey as the original wisher," whatever that meant. Maybe that would help stop these "coincidences."

X   *I wish the dentist will not have to pull my two back molars for braces.*

X   *I wish my new school smells like warm chocolate chip cookies.*

X   *I wish when it stops raining that no soggy worms will fry on the sidewalk the next sunny day.*

?   *I wish to become an amazing bass guitarist.*

?   *I wish for a baby sister.*

?   *I wish for Grandma Penshine to get well soon.*

?   *I wish no kid in the world has nasty green food caught in his teeth and no one tells him.*

In her left pocket was the "no homework" penny, and in her right pocket was the "world peace" penny.

Griffin couldn't stop touching the pennies. The natural oil from her palms was making them glow. No homework and world peace seemed nearly impossible, so she decided to start with them. Even on math tests Griffin always attacked the hardest problems first.

"See you after science. We'll save a seat for you at lunch," said Libby, with Maggie Hart and Madison James, friends from elementary school, heading toward their social studies class. Griffin continued walking alone down the long science wing, past bulletin boards of colored paper, past the stingy water fountain that doled out a droplet at a time, and into the huge science room with cardboard planets dangling from the ceiling.

A few kids sat in their seats, staring at the planets slowly swaying back and forth as if they were on a hypnotist's chain. Griffin took her seat.

"Good morning, my bright and amazing students, the future scientists of the universe! We are here to understand THE WORLD! THE ENTIRE SOLAR SYSTEM! THE UNIVERSE!" said Mr. Luckner, the sixth-grade science teacher. He wore yellow pants and a black shirt with puffy planets dancing all over it. "Can you all believe at this very minute that at the equator our planet is spinning one thousand thirty-eight miles per *hour*? The average speed for a car on the highway is fifty-five miles per hour! Think about how fast the earth is moving right now! Dizzy, anyone?"

The boys in the back row kept staring at the cardboard planets, heads swaying.

"We all should be dizzy just thinking about it!"

A few kids yawned as some others quickly tried to finish their homework while Mr. Luckner wasn't looking.

"All-righty! How many minutes would it take a rocket to travel from Earth into space?"

Griffin's hand shot up. "Nine minutes!" she blurted out.

"Very good, Griffin, very good," said Mr. Luckner. Griffin knew this because her mom always said, when stuck in holiday traffic, "I can't believe this! In a rocket we could reach *outer space* in nine minutes and we're stuck in Dadesville County traffic for thirty minutes!"

Griffin smiled, thinking about her mom. A boy she didn't know, Zeke, at the desk next to her smiled back. Giant chunks of green spinach snarled in his braces. A girl sitting to her left, Ashley, smiled. Green goop stuck in her front braces too.

Griffin's eyes grew huge. That was another of her wishes: *I wish no kid in the world has nasty green food caught in his braces and no one tells him.*

I have to tell them! she thought. "Zeke!" she whispered. "Zeke!"

Mr. Luckner called, "Griffin, would you come to the board and try to estimate how long it would take to travel from Earth to Jupiter if I gave you some facts?"

"Okay," said Griffin, distracted by the spinach.

She walked toward the front of the class. Mr. Luckner handed her a dry erase marker, and she climbed up on one of the high stools to write the formula on the whiteboard. Just as she placed her foot on the inner rim of the stool, her penny tumbled out of her pocket and rolled on the floor like a wobbly planet, in front of the whole class.

Mr. Luckner swooped down to pick it up before she could climb off the stool. "Find a penny, pick it up, all day long you'll have good luck," sang Mr. Luckner, turning the penny over in his hand.

"'No homework,'" he read.

Griffin stood in front of him. The whole class hushed.

"Griffin, are you trying to send me a message?" he asked.

"No. It's just a penny I found," she answered.

A strange look washed over Mr. Luckner's face. "A penny that has 'no homework' taped on it!" said Mr. Luckner. A stillness engulfed the room, and even the swinging planets stopped. The science room snake flicked its tongue against the glass wall of its terrarium. Its yellow eyes lit up, glaring at Griffin. Mr. Luckner stared, mesmerized by the penny. Light from the penny blinded the entire class.

Mr. Luckner exploded, "THIS IS A MARVELOUS idea! A stupendous idea! NO HOMEWORK!"

Every kid in the room sat up, electrified.

"Instead . . . ," said Mr. Luckner. A strange glow emanated from the penny and scattered light off the hanging planets. A copper radiance swirled in Mr. Luckner's eyes. Mr. Luckner spoke again. "Instead of nightly homework for the next month, I'm assigning all of you participation in our school's science night. In the past, science night was voluntary for sixth graders, but it is now *mandatory* for all of you! You will create a booth, display materials, and write a six-page paper to present at science night. You must work on this using books and the Internet. You have a little less than one month to get ready for science night.

"My whole life I've been wishing for no homework to correct!" said Mr. Luckner, and he tossed the penny back to Griffin—but just then a gust of air swept through the room, flinging the penny into the tropical fish tank.

Griffin watched the penny sink through the aquarium water, past the sharp red coral, and disappear into a plastic sunken ship. All the fish bulged their fish eyeballs, circling around and around in pursuit of the lost penny.

"Your first quarter science grade will depend on your science night booth and your oral reports on a famous scientist, due next week," said Mr. Luckner.

He wrote on the board:

Wednesday, September 10, ORAL REPORTS (on famous scientists)

Wednesday, September 24, SCIENCE NIGHT (booth and paper)

"That's all folks. No homework! Just two projects this month. No more nightly correcting for me! Brilliant idea, Griffin!"

"Now look at all the work we have to do!" said Zeke. Green vegetables stuck in his braces.

"I'm excited!" said Audree Stein, who had long chocolate brown hair that fell in soft waves around her pretty heart-shaped face.

"I'm not! Thanks for ruining the first month of school!" said Michael Janis.

Griffin bit down hard on her lower lip. She thought, *This is how the first wish begins.*

✳ ✳ ✳

Be careful what you wish for.

Chapter
11

H ow's school going, Griff?" asked her dad when
he picked her up at car pool.

"Fine," she said, but school had been any-
thing but fine the last three days. Kids in Mr. Luckner's class
were angry at having to do a science project, and she'd found
more and more pieces of toilet paper stuck in her locker. She
slid the "world peace" penny deep into her pocket for the
whole world's safety.

"Really?" said her dad, knowing her too well. He pulled
onto the main road headed to the bakery in the center of town.

"I guess it's just getting used to a new school," said Griffin.

* * *

When they entered the bakery, smells of cupcakes and melting chocolate greeted them. "Would you like a sample?" asked the lady behind the counter, holding out a frosted double chocolate brownie to Griffin and her dad.

"Just what I was wishing for, Griff!" said her dad, licking the chocolate from his fingers like a little boy.

"Yeah," Griffin said, and she smiled sadly. She wanted to tell her dad so badly about Mariah.

"We're here to pick up a cake for my wife's baby shower," he said.

"Oh, yes, we're almost done frosting Saturn's rings. Can you give us five minutes?" asked the clerk.

"Sure," said her dad, spying the newspaper rack.

"Dad, I'm going to go outside and look at the cakes in the window."

"Okay, Griff."

In the large refrigerated bakery window, rose petals were scattered on the floor of the case. Three cakes of different shapes rested on stands. One was shaped like a race car, another heart-shaped with strawberries and raspberries on top, and the largest cake of all frosted a perfect pink. A beautiful porcelain figure of a ballerina twirled on top of it.

A few feet from Griffin a tall, willowy girl, whom Griffin recognized from gym class, stopped with her mother to look in the bakery window. "Look, Mom," said the girl. "Look at the cake with the ballerina! She's beautiful! Can I please, please, *please* take ballet lessons?"

"Kristina, I told you, it's a waste of money," said her mom.

"How do you know?" Kristina asked.

"Only one percent of ballet dancers can even get a job or make a living."

"What if I'm the one percent?" asked Kristina.

"Most people aren't meant to be dancers; they're meant to watch. Lessons are a lot of money, and then for what?"

"Mom—"

"The answer is no!" said her mom. "Come on. I'm going to get a parking ticket!" Kristina's mom walked away.

"I know I could be the most beautiful dancer if I took lessons, Mom," called Kristina to her mother's back.

Griffin froze.

Most beautiful rang in Griffin's ears. *That's one of the wishes,* she thought. She turned to look at Kristina.

Kristina slunk a few paces behind her mother.

Griffin went back inside the bakery. A giant cake was set on the counter in the shape of Saturn, its rings frosted in yellow, orange, and red. The frosted letters on top read, *Congratulations! We're over the moon (s) for you!*

Griffin smiled. Saturn had more than sixty moons, so

the writing was a special joke for the people who worked at the observatory. "It's not every woman who would want a Saturn-shaped cake," said her dad, laughing.

The bakery door flung open behind them. Samantha, Sasha, and Martha strutted right past Griffin, pretending not to see her. At the counter Samantha said to the saleswoman, "I'm here to pick up my forty chocolate chip cookie invitations to my birthday party."

Glancing down at the Saturn cake, Samantha whispered to her friends, "Nerd cake! Maybe they should serve it with *toilet paper.*"

Sasha and Martha laughed.

Griffin stared at the three girls and mumbled under her breath, "I wish Samantha looked like a queen lizard with warts all over her face!" Griffin gasped. What a horrible thing to wish . . . even on Samantha! Her chest felt tight, her throat went dry . . . as if dark tentacles coiled inside her.

"We'd better hurry, Griffin," said her dad.

"I know," she said.

Inside Dadesville's domed planetarium a galaxy of millions of stars was projected against the darkening blue sky. The Pleiades, Betelgeuse, Sirius, Pegasus, Orion's Belt, Ursa Major, and Hercules all shined in the dimming heavens. Even

Cygnus, the swan, soared on the giant ceiling above them.

Griffin sat alone in one of the reclining chairs looking up at the universe. From the bottom of her backpack she took out the box of pennies and hid them under her coat. Penny number one, "no homework," had not gone well at all. How had it fallen out of her pocket when she had stuck it deep inside the cotton lining?

Griffin peered into Mariah's black box. Slowly she studied the different pennies. She had slid the "world peace" penny back into its slot. Griffin held a penny up to the faded ceiling starlight. The label was curling off. It said "success." "Success?" she whispered. Griffin's grandma said she had a great success every time her garden bloomed in the spring. Was success qualifying for the Olympic team, having a true friend, or being a great parent?

"Please, please, please," she whispered, "to all my old and favorite stars my mom taught me, help guide me to return these stolen wishes."

✳ ✳ ✳

When it is dark enough, men see stars.
—Ralph Waldo Emerson

Chapter

12

The next day in Mr. Luckner's class, Griffin watched the planets swish on the wire above her desk. Mr. Luckner gave the class some time to work on their projects in class, but kids just slumped in their seats and chatted. Griffin tried to cheer herself up. She had returned the "no homework" wish, and maybe something good would come of it. David Hunt tugged a strand of Griffin's hair from his desk behind her. He teased, "Girls go to Jupiter . . ."

Griffin whirled around. "David, you're saying it all wrong. It's 'Girls go to Mars to become rock stars.'"

"Yeah, right. Girl rock stars stink," said David.

"Dude, there are some amazing girl rock stars: Janis Joplin, Michelle Shocked, Tina Weymouth," said Garrett, flipping his moppy bangs as he walked past their desks.

How can he see under all that hair? Griffin wondered.

"How do you know so much about music?" she asked.

"I'm in a band," he said proudly.

"Really? That's so cool. What's the name of your band?"

"Excuse me," said Mr. Luckner. "This is work time, not social hour. Everybody is so busy chitchatting that it seems you all prefer partners. Okay, class, it's TEAM PROJECTS, then! You all must earn a grade together! My two As, Audree and Aiden—a team! Brian and Brent . . . Garrett and Griffin . . ."

"Come on, no, Mr. Luckner, please!" some students begged if they were unhappy with their partners. On the other hand, people who got hardworking partners couldn't stop smiling.

Garrett beamed.

Griffin cringed.

She couldn't imagine working with Garrett for the next month. Although half the girls already had crushes on him, with his crazy hair and twinkling blue eyes, Griffin noticed how he doodled nonstop in every class they were in together.

Garrett stood over her desk.

"Have you started a project or picked an idea?" asked Griffin.

"Yeah. It's practically finished." Garrett shrugged and tossed his hair out of his face.

"Really?" said Griffin, shocked. She hadn't even decided on a topic yet. Trying to concentrate on anything was difficult with the weight of those wishes upon her.

"What have you done?"

"It's done in my head," he said.

The bell rang.

After ripping off a piece of her notebook paper, she wrote down her number. "Can you call me tonight? We can decide on a project, divide up the work, and set some times to meet at the library. Science night is a huge grade, Garrett. It's really important to me. My mom's a scientist and . . ."

"Yeah," said Garrett, smiling like he'd just won the lottery. "It's *way* important to me, too!" He walked out of class and hummed, "Girls go to Mars . . ."

On the way to lunch after gym class, Griffin noticed a slumped figure hunched by the water fountain in the hallway. It was the girl Griffin had seen in front of the bakery the day before. "Kristina?" called Griffin.

When Kristina turned around, her face was swollen like she had been crying all night. "Are you okay?" asked Griffin.

"Yeah," she said, not meeting Griffin's eyes.

"I'm Griffin. You were amazing during the fitness tests today!"

A tiny smile pulled on Kristina's lips.

"You know, I saw you at the town bakery yesterday," said Griffin.

"Oh, yeah?" she said, shrinking with embarrassment.

"I heard you say you loved ballet." Now Griffin blushed at what she was about to say.

Just then Mr. Luckner walked past them, whistling to himself. Griffin wondered if she was doing the right thing at all. Taking a deep breath, she continued. "I have something for you," said Griffin, digging into her backpack.

"Really?" said Kristina.

"This is a very old lucky penny. Maybe you could be the most beautiful dancer if you wished on it," said Griffin in one hurried, embarrassed breath.

Kristina took the penny and read, "most beautiful" on the tiny tag glued across the penny.

Quickly Griffin swiveled her head to see if anyone was watching.

"What do I do with it?" asked Kristina.

Gurgling water surging inside the water fountain pipes gave Griffin an idea. Griffin knew water conducted electricity. Maybe if the penny were dunked in water it could reenergize its original wish. "You should wash it off, *recharge* it, and make a 'most beautiful' something wish. Be specific, then wait until it comes true."

Kristina probably would have thought it silly, holding the penny under the trickling water fountain, if it weren't such a miraculous-looking penny. "This penny is psychedelic!" She swished the dripping wet penny in her palm, squeezed her fingers around it, and mumbled her wish. Light surged out between Kristina's fingers.

BAAANGGGG!

Griffin jumped.

Kristina's hand jerked open. A locker slammed in a distant hallway.

"Oh, no!" Kristina cried.

"What?" said Griffin, looking down the empty hallway.

"The penny! I just dropped the penny down the water fountain drain!" Kristina's face started to turn blotchy.

Griffin stared at the water fountain. "That's okay, Kristina. Uhh, it's exactly what was supposed to happen! How could I have forgotten to tell you?" said Griffin, thinking fast. "After you wish, you need to throw the penny into water for the magic to travel. Usually it's a well, but the school water fountain is just fine." Griffin wiped her sweaty palms on her jeans.

A second locker door slammed and Samantha Sloane, carrying a stack of huge chocolate chip cookie invitations, slunk toward Griffin and Kristina.

"What are you guys doing? Why did you just give Kristina that penny?" demanded Samantha. "Are you *paying* kids to be friends with you?"

"What?" said Griffin.

"Griffin was just—," said Kristina.

"NO! Don't tell, Kristina!" said Griffin.

"Thanks. Gotta go!" Kristina said, and she ran down the hall.

Griffin stood face-to-face with Samantha. "Don't tell me what?" asked Samantha, her teeth glinting in the fluorescent hall light.

"None of your business," said Griffin, meeting her stare.

"Hey, Griffin!" said Garrett, walking up to them. "What's your number again? I lost it, but I'll call tonight," he said. "Here, I'll write it on my arm so I don't forget."

Samantha's eyes grew narrower and narrower as Griffin told her number to Garrett.

"Passing out pennies and your number, *Griff*?" she said.

"Science project, *Sam*," Griffin shot right back.

Suddenly Samantha swirled around and flashed her eyes like a lit-up slot machine at Garrett. "Hey, Garrett," she purred. "I wanted to give you one of my chocolate chip cookie invitations to my birthday party this Saturday." She handed over the frosted cookie with her address and the time of the party.

Samantha's B-day
Sat. 9/6
1:00 PM
408 Rosmell Court

"Cool cookie!" he said, taking a bite out of the time and address. Now it read:

Samantha's B-day!
at. 9/6
00 PM
smell Court

Griffin read the mangled cookie and smiled.

"I hope you come," Samantha flirted.

"Thanks," said Garrett, taking another bite of the cookie as he walked away. "Later."

Samantha whirled back to face Griffin. Just then Samantha's two best friends ran up to her. Martha, who always looked like she stepped out of a designer accessory catalog, said, "We just passed out another twelve cookies, and so far everyone is saying *yes*!" They high-fived and giggled.

"Your party is going to be amazing!" said Sasha.

"With only the coolest people invited," said Martha, ignoring Griffin.

"I know," said Samantha, and they strutted down the hall with smirks on their faces.

* * *

No pessimist ever discovered the secret of the stars
or sailed an uncharted land,
or opened a new doorway for the human spirit.
—Helen Keller

Chapter 13

Jamming on her bass guitar in her bedroom after school, with her headphones on, Griffin slashed at the strings and pounded her head to the raging music. She hated Samantha's clique. *Did it really look like I was paying kids to be friends with me, bringing presents for people I'd just met?* thought Griffin. Griffin's back hurt. Her head hurt. Everything hurt.

"GRIFF! GRIFF!" yelled her mother outside her room. "GRIFFIN!" Her mom knocked on her door.

Griffin jumped down from her bed and opened her door.

Her mother put her hand on her hip and stared. "What's going on? Didn't you hear me?"

"Sorry, Mom. My music was too loud."

"Is everything okay?" she asked.

"Yeah," Griffin said with a shrug, avoiding her mom's eyes.

"I've been calling you. The phone has been ringing off the hook," said her mom, holding the phone in her hand. "Libby called and said call her right back. She has to tell you something really important. Also the dentist called and said she made a mistake. She said she was looking at the wrong X-rays. She doesn't have to pull your back molars after all, and a Garrett Forester called."

Did Griffin just hear her mother right? The dentist didn't have to pull her molars? Her wish had come true! Maybe giving the "no homework" penny to Mr. Luckner had done something good! Maybe she could do it. Maybe there was a way to stop the curse. Griffin jumped up and down, ran up to her bed, and cartwheeled off. "NO WAY!" she shouted. "I CAN'T BELIEVE IT! I AM SOOOO HAPPY!"

Griffin's mother stared. "Is this because that Garrett boy called?"

"WHAT?" said Griffin, stopping mid-cartwheel. "No! Oh, my gosh, Mom, no! I just can't believe that the dentist said she doesn't have to pull my molars. You don't understand!" Griffin twirled around the room again.

"I guess not," said her mom, staring at Griffin oddly. "Who is this boy?"

"Mom, please! Garrett is my science partner for science night. We got assigned to work together."

"Okay," said her mom, still staring.

"I better call Libby back! Thanks, Mom!" said Griffin, now dancing around her room. *It worked!* She didn't have to have her back molars pulled! Maybe giving Mr. Luckner the penny counted! Her intention had been sincere to help Kristina, too. Maybe Kristina could be the "most beautiful" dancer and another of Griffin's own wishes would come true! She couldn't believe how Kristina's mom had talked to her about dancing— just like a Wish Stealer. She could never imagine her parents talking to her like that, stomping on her dreams.

I'm on a roll! she thought. Griffin cartwheeled off her bed again. *I refuse to be a Wish Stealer! Take that, Mariah!* Another cartwheel made her dizzy. *Then again,* Griffin thought, *if it's working, that means I need to return more wishes so the opposite of my other wishes won't come true!* Griffin remembered her wish for her grandma to get well. She thought of the new baby on the way. She had to work even faster to return the wishes.

"You're growing up, Griff," said her mom, all teary-eyed, watching her from the doorway.

"Mom, please!"

Just then the telephone rang.

"Forester Garrett," read Griffin's mom off the caller ID. "He's calling again?"

"Mom, it's a science project! I gotta take this." Griffin took the phone from her mom's hand, waved good-bye, closed the door, and flopped onto her bed.

"Hello?"

"Griffin, hi, it's Garrett. Sorry, I was going to leave a message 'cause my mom and I are going out for pizza."

"Yeah, thanks for calling. We need to pick a science project idea. I have a couple ideas."

"Maybe we could blow something up, show how explosions work, or grow something really gnarly," said Garrett.

"Huh," said Griffin, thinking. *Maybe we could make a force field against Samantha?* she thought. But instead she said, "Can you meet me at the town library after school tomorrow? We can look at some books and decide on a topic. I can talk more with my parents tonight about it, okay?"

"Okay," he said, "but I gotta be quick. Band practice."

"Cool," said Griffin, feeling her face getting warm.

"Griffin, are you coming? Dinner's ready," called her mom.

"Garrett, I gotta go eat dinner," she said.

"All right," he said. "Bye."

"Bye," she said, surprised her heart was beating so fast.

Quickly Griffin dialed Libby. "Hey, Libbs, what's up?"

"I have the most unbelievable news ever! But first, I think Garrett Forester totally likes you. Audree agrees with me. She said he totally flirted with you in science class."

"What?" said Griffin, blushing again alone in her room.

"He smiled at you twice by your locker! I know he thought the picture of you playing bass was supercool," said Libby.

"Libby, I was standing in a puddle of toilet paper! Who wouldn't be smiling?" said Griffin.

"Trust me," said Libby.

Griffin shook her head. Just as she was about to tell Libby that Garrett had called, Libby said, "Anyway, I just heard that Samantha did *not* win the Fresh Face contest because she broke out in an unexplained rash on her face right before the finals! She has bumps all over her face that look like lizard skin!"

Griffin's heart plunged. Suddenly she remembered the horrible wish that had popped into her head at the bakery when Samantha had called her mom's cake a "nerd cake." *I wish Samantha looked like a queen lizard with warts all over her face!*

Oh, no! thought Griffin, sinking into her bed. Samantha

was cruel, but Griffin hadn't really meant for her to break out in warts. Had she? Griffin ran to the mirror and looked at herself. Her eyes had an odd yellow tint . . . like Mariah's.

"Griffin, are you there?" said Libby.

"Yeah. Sorry, Libbs, my mom's calling me for dinner."

"Okay. But isn't this just like in English class? *Something wicked this way comes!*"

"Yeah. Something wicked. See you tomorrow."

Griffin clutched herself. Had one of her hurtful wishes come true? She thought back to Mariah's letter. *If you are a Wish Stealer, only your evil wishes will come true.*

Griffin lurched under her bed, scooped up the amethyst stone for protection, put it into her pocket, and went downstairs for dinner.

"Is everything all right, Griff?" asked her mom when she sat at the table.

"Yeah," she said.

"Who is this Garrett?" asked her dad.

"Mr. Luckner made Garrett and me partners for our science night project. The only problem is that I get the feeling that Garrett doesn't do any homework. Is it okay if I walk next door to the town library after school tomorrow to meet him? Then can you pick me up when I'm done?"

"Okay. Just call when you want me to get you. Do you have any science project ideas? I used to love science fairs when I was in school," said her mom, smiling.

"That's because you won them all," her dad said with a laugh.

"I really want to do something about the environment," said Griffin. "Garrett wants to grow something weird or blow something up."

Across the table Griffin's parents raised their eyebrows at each other.

✳ ✳ ✳

Make a wish together
and change the world.

Chapter

14

At school the next day Samantha came in with a thick coat of makeup on her face, looking deeply tan or orange, depending on the light.

Griffin gulped.

Samantha, Martha, and Sasha passed out reminders for her birthday party, sticking chocolate chip cookie magnets on the invited kids' lockers.

Walking by Kristina, Griffin heard her mumble under her breath, "I'm never invited to cool things."

Another girl cried when every locker surrounding hers had a chocolate chip cookie magnet on it except hers. "Whoa," said Robert Winbell, passing by Samantha, "you wear more makeup than my grandma."

"It's called a tanning bed," said Samantha. "You are so not invited to my party."

Griffin narrowed her eyes. She started to wish the party was ruined or no one showed up—*NO, NO, NO, I DO NOT WISH THAT! Do I?* thought Griffin.

How easy it was to wish awful things when she was upset.

Griffin tried to focus on making it through the school day and meeting Garrett at the town library instead.

Griffin spread five books across the library table. Garrett was nowhere in sight. She checked her watch. For fifteen minutes she had been waiting, and she wondered if he'd remember, even though she'd reminded him in science class. Walking toward the library computers, Griffin spotted Garrett sitting on the floor between two bookshelves, reading a guitar magazine.

"Garrett," she said. "I thought you forgot."

"Hey, Griffin," he said. "No, I got here twenty minutes ago. Just getting some ideas. Never been here before. It's pretty neat. I mean, man, I found some wild stuff."

"*Band Magazine*?" she read aloud, standing over him. "What's that?"

"Just reading about this band called the Austin Alchemists—got their name from wizards or something," he said.

"Can I see?" Griffin asked. Garrett stood up and gave her the magazine.

She read aloud from the article interviewing the lead singer. "'We got our band's name after the ancient alchemists who were, like, radical wizard scientists, man. They tried to find a secret formula to turn lead into gold. Just like we're gonna get a gold record when our CD sells a million copies!'"

"Cool," said Garrett. "If I could make gold, I'd buy my mom all the stuff she ever wanted."

Griffin continued reading the interview, "'Alchemy was like the bridge, this awesomely long bridge between superstitions and modern science. Our band is, like, modern, man.' I never heard of their band. But maybe Mr. Luckner would let us do our project about turning ordinary metals into gold."

"'This could be so cool!" said Garrett. "Maybe we could do an experiment at the science fair. Blow all the kids away! Like take a penny and turn it into gold!"

Like turning a penny into a wish, thought Griffin, but she didn't say that aloud.

"Let's ask a librarian for help, okay?" she said, leading Garrett to the information desk.

Mrs. Eve, the nicest librarian in the library, happened to be at the help desk. With her huge smile, sparkling eyes, and framed photo of her new baby on the counter, kids felt like they could ask her anything.

"Hi, Mrs. Eve," Griffin said.

"Hi, Griff. Great to see you. Looks like you brought a friend," she said smiling.

"This is my science partner, Garrett."

"Hi, Garrett. Nice to meet you," said Mrs. Eve.

"Hi," said Garrett.

"We're looking for info about the ancient alchemists," said Griffin. "It might be a totally weird topic . . ."

Mrs. Eve said, "Weird? Not at all! Ancient alchemy is one of the most fascinating topics you could research. Turning lead into gold, the transmutation of ugly things into beauty—the study of alchemy is a great choice! Let's go to the ancient books section. All of our oldest and most valuable books are locked up down there."

She reached for a huge loop of keys behind the counter. Down two creaky flights of stairs, Garrett and Griffin followed behind Mrs. Eve. Underground caverns of books appeared in long rows stretching like a silent city beneath the library.

"I never knew this existed," said Griffin. Sounds of a metal door being unlocked echoed through the crypt of books.

"Ancient Alchemy," said Mrs. Eve, pointing to the last row of books by the wall. "Amazing things inside. You two may never want to leave!"

"Thanks," said Garrett and Griffin at the same time.

WISH! she wanted to shout, but bit her tongue instead. She didn't even want to think about that.

Just then the phone rang inside the ancient book vault. Mrs. Eve reached to answer it. "Hello?" she said. "I'll be right there." She hung up the receiver and said to Garrett and Griffin, "I have to run. We usually don't let people unsupervised down here, but, Griffin, I've known you and your family for years." She smiled at them. "I'll be back in ten minutes, okay?"

Griffin nodded her head. "Thank you so much." Mrs. Eve's footsteps echoed through the silent underground room as she walked up the stairs.

Griffin stared at Garrett when the door slammed. They were left alone.

"Cool," said Garrett. He pulled a giant book from the shelf. "*The Dictionary of Ancient Alchemy, 1785.*"

The book weighed a ton. Dust flew off it like a poisonous cloud. Garrett opened the antique book and placed it on a reading stand set up at the end of a bookcase. Griffin and Garrett stood side by side in front of the book. Garrett read,

"'We start with *Z*. Zosimos of Panopolis.'" His voice bounced off the walls of the tomblike room.

"It's kinda creepy down here, don't you think?" said Griffin.

"Not really. I stay at home by myself all the time," replied Garrett, shrugging. "Look at this!" He continued reading. "'Zosimos, called the father of alchemy, believed only *four* metals could be changed into gold.'"

"What are the four metals?" asked Griffin, now centimeters away from Garrett.

"'Lead, tin, silver, and copper,'" read Garrett.

"Copper!" said Griffin, leaning her head over the book. Her long, shiny hair brushed the page.

"'Maria Prophetissa, the most famous woman alchemist, made the first laboratory equipment. It was called a *tribikos*, to make gold,'" she read excitedly.

"Your hair smells like strawberries," said Garrett.

"Really?" said Griffin, jerking her head away.

Garret and Griffin stared at each other across the book, and they both blushed at the same time.

"I—I guess it's my shampoo," she said, her face now bright red like a giant strawberry.

Do I have green food stuck in my teeth? thought Griffin, and she suddenly became self-conscious. Quickly she looked down and continued reading. "'Basil Valentine, said to have lived in Paris in 1394, believed in the properties of a metal called antimony. This strange, poisonous metal fascinated Isaac Newton.'"

"Look at that," said Garrett, pointing to a picture. A black shiny circle was drawn on the next page. He read, "'This circular black ob-sid-i-an mirror can be seen today in the British Museum. It was believed to have been stolen from Aztec priests by the conquistadors, who transported it to Europe. This magic mirror was used by the ancient alchemists to see the future.'"

Griffin glued her eyes to the page. The magic mirror was just like the one she'd seen in Mr. Schmidt's shop.

※　　※　　※

Turn something ordinary
into something extraordinary.

Chapter

15

Six times the town bell rang outside, reminding Garrett and Griffin they had been researching for two hours. "Wow! That went by fast," he said. Pushing through the heavy wooden doors, they emerged into the library's front courtyard, each with a stack of books.

"CDs! Buy your violin CD here," called a sad-looking sidewalk musician standing by the flagpole. In one hand he clutched his violin and bow, in the other he held up his self-produced CD for sale. Before him lay a stack of unsold CDs and an open violin case. Not a single coin had been tossed inside. People walked in and out of the library and passed by him as if he were a lamppost. With his head bowed to the ground, he picked up his violin. Slowly he played a haunting, melancholy song. Griffin stared.

"Griffin?" said Garrett. "You okay?"

"Yeah. His violin case is empty," she said.

"What are you going to do?" Garrett said. "Give him some leftover lunch money?"

When the violinist stopped playing, Griffin walked up to the forlorn man. Although he wasn't that old, his face sagged. "You play really great."

"Thanks," he said, not meeting her eyes.

"I play bass guitar."

"Good for you. Hope you don't end up a failure like me."

Griffin's mouth fell open. "You're not a failure," she said. "Your music sounds incredible!"

The man smiled sadly.

"Griff! I'm parked right here," called Dr. Penshine from the open car window.

"I gotta go," she said, turning to Garrett. "That's my mom. Do you need a ride home?"

"No, I'm gonna walk," he said.

"Don't you have band practice like you said on the phone?" asked Griffin.

"Nah, we bailed," said Garrett.

"Okay. Well, we got a lot done. Thanks. See you tomorrow," she said.

"Tomorrow's Saturday," he said, and smiled.

"Oh, yeah." She blushed.

"Hey, are you going to Samantha's party?" he asked.

"Uh, no. I . . . ," she said.

"Yeah, it will probably be lame. I ate that cookie anyway." Griffin laughed.

Garrett smiled at her again.

"Griffin!" called her mom.

"Gotta go," she said, running to the car and slipping into the front seat.

"Hi," said her mom. "Is that Garrett over there?" Her mom pointed to Garrett, who was talking to the sidewalk musician.

"Yes," Griffin said.

"Does he want to have dinner with us?" her mom asked.

"Who?" Griffin said.

"Garrett," said her mom.

"I don't think so."

"How is he getting home?" asked her mom.

"He said he's walking," said Griffin, staring out the window.

"At night? By himself? I don't think so!" said her mom.

"Why don't we eat across the street at Friendly's? Dad's working late. Maybe Garrett would like to have dinner with us? I can drop him off afterward."

"It's okay, really," Griffin said.

"He shouldn't be walking home in the dark," her mom persisted.

"All right," Griffin said. She got out of the car and walked up to Garrett. "Hey, Garrett. Do you want to go to Friendly's with us? Then my mom can drop you off."

"Friendly's?" he said with a huge smile. "I love their Reese's Pieces sundae."

"Yeah," said Griffin.

"Okay," he said.

Settled into the restaurant booth, Dr. Penshine asked Garrett, "Do you want to call your parents and let them know you're eating with us?"

"It's okay. My mom works late most nights, so she won't even know the difference."

"Does your dad work late too?" said Griffin.

"He doesn't live with us," said Garrett, studying the menu.

"Where does he live?" asked Griffin.

Garrett shrugged his shoulders and shifted uneasily.

"Alaska. He's a fisherman. Hey, the double-decker looks awe-some!"

Clanking dishes and clinking glasses spun circles around Griffin.

"What can I get you all?" asked the waitress, chewing gum.

"A double-decker and Reese's Pieces sundae," said Garrett.

"All-righty," said the waitress. "And you, young lady?"

But Griffin just stared at Garrett.

"Griffin, the waitress is talking to you," said her mom, raising an eyebrow.

"Sorry. A veggie burger, please," she said, returning her focus to Garrett. "Have you ever *wished* for your dad to come back, Garrett?"

"Griffin!" said her mom. "That's a very personal question!"

"It's okay," said Garrett. "I don't care. He left two years ago. I was ten. I used to wish on my birthday cake for him to come back. But now that I'm older, I don't wish for such stupid things."

"I don't think it's a stupid wish at all, Garrett. I know lots of people who have wished for amazing things! Crazy things!" said Griffin, leaning across the table.

Cackling laughter caught Griffin's ear from a few booths

away. In full costume the three witches from *Macbeth* gnawed on chicken bones, with spinach and chicken flapping in their teeth.

"Oh, my gosh," gasped Griffin, spotting them. "It's the witches!"

"Who?" said her mom.

"What?" said Garrett.

Griffin's heart raced.

One of the witches noticed Griffin staring at her. She waved her bony fingers and called to her, "'In the cauldron boil and bake . . . *Lizard's* leg and owlet's wing . . .' Right, my dear? 'For a charm of powerful trouble.'"

"My goodness, they look lifelike," said Griffin's mom.

"They performed for my English class. Actors from some traveling theater company doing *Macbeth*," Griffin said, and gulped.

"Gnarly!" said Garrett.

"I'd love to hear what you two picked for your science night project," said Dr. Penshine, changing the subject.

"Alchemy! Turning lead into gold!" said Garrett.

Just then the three witches left their table, heading for the exit. As they passed Griffin's table, one of the hags leaned over and whispered, "'When the hurlyburly's done, / When the battle's lost and won,' ehh, my dear?"

The crone's eyes swirled yellow.

When the three weird witches exited the restaurant, a cold gust of wind snuck through the doors.

"What does that mean?" Griffin asked her mom, shivering.

"I think it's a line from the play. 'Hurlyburly' means everything's upside down, lots of confusion. My goodness, those are either the oddest or most committed actors I have ever seen! They must be in character rehearsing their parts," she said.

"What does the second line mean?" asked Garrett.

"'When the battle's lost and won'? I think it means someone emerges victorious from a battle between good and evil."

✳ ✳ ✳

Turn a single penny into gold.

Chapter
16

Right here," said Garrett as the Penshines' car pulled up in front of a small, dark house without a single light on.

"Good night, Garrett. It was nice to meet you," said Dr. Penshine. "Quite an evening, a real dinner theater experience with those actors!"

"Bye," said Griffin, her eyes scanning the darkness around his house. *Why did the witch say that to me?* she thought.

"Yeah, thanks for dinner," said Garrett, shutting the car door.

They waved through the window and watched as Garrett

traipsed down the broken cement path to his house, netted in shadows.

"You know, Griff, when I was at the counter paying for dinner, the clerk gave me back a bunch of pennies."

"Yeah?" Griffin said. She couldn't stop thinking about the witches. What did they mean "when the battle's lost and won"? *What will I lose if I fail?*

"Are you okay?" asked her mom, studying her in the passing streetlights.

"What were you saying about pennies?" Griffin asked, eyes darting. *Did my mom find Mariah's note under my bed?*

"They reminded me of something that might help your alchemy project. There's a charity called Pennies for the Planet." Dr. Penshine rounded the corner, and a streetlight flickered on. "This charity helps protect the environment. Every year the projects change, but this year I think kids are collecting pennies to buy an acre of the rain forest. This saves it from being destroyed.

"All those ordinary pennies turn into something extraordinary when they're added together, like the alchemists turning lead into gold."

"That's a really cool idea, Mom. I'll text Garrett about it," said Griffin.

The car hovered at a red light.

When the hurlyburly's done, when the battle's lost and won screeched in Griffin's head. *Can I return all these wishes?*

Courage is . . . mastery of fear, not absence of fear.

—Mark Twain

Chapter

The art store on Saturday morning glowed with sunlight streaming in its windows. Neat rows of paints in silver tubes waited like dignified soldiers to be purchased. Brushes in every shape and size tickled the shelves above them. Griffin and Libby loved to come here to buy a few new supplies before heading to Grandma Penshine's house for their art lesson. In the afternoon, when the weatherman predicted the temperature would hit eighty-five degrees, they'd meet Audree, Maggie, and Madison to swim in Maggie's grandpa's pool.

"My grandma says today she's teaching us about the Venetian painters, so we should pick out our favorite blues and yellows to paint an amazing sky," said Griffin as they looked through the rack of paint colors.

"Cobalt blue, azure mist, lapis lazuli, Caspian Sea blue, aquamarine, cerulean swirl," read Libby as she carefully examined each tube. "How many blues can there be in the world?"

Just then a breeze blew through the store, and five girls, babbling loudly, some on their cell phones, others laughing, burst through the art store's doors.

"Grab every color. My father said he'd pay for everything. We want my birthday party banner to be huge! We'll drape it across my house so everyone will know which house to come to!" said a familiar voice.

Griffin turned as Samantha and her followers surged around the paint rack, trying to bump her and Libby out of the way.

"Excuse you," said Griffin, refusing to be pushed.

"What are you two doing here?" Samantha snickered.

"We're buying paints for our art lesson," said Libby.

"Do you guys think you're going to be famous artists one day? Now, that's hilarious!"

"They are so not invited to Samantha's party," Martha whispered loudly as she ripped paint tubes from the metal shelves and put them into a basket.

"Totally," said Sasha. "They're probably here because they heard we were coming to the art store and they're hoping to be invited. Desperate!"

"We only have three hours before my party. Come on. We want my sign to be gigantic!" Like a writhing octopus with groping arms on all sides of the paint display, the girls grabbed at the lapis, cobalt, and aquamarine. Soon the Caspian Sea blue, cerulean swirl, and azure mist were all snatched away too.

"Hey, you guys can't take them all!" said Griffin, reaching to protect some paints.

A windmill of arms slapped the space in front of her. Griffin's eyes narrowed in disgust. The entire rack of paint was stripped, except for one fallen soldier of *triste bleu*, and that was only because no one in Samantha's clique could read French.

"Hurry, girls! My older sister is going to take us to drop off some extra chocolate chip cookie invitations at the boys' houses. Boys always need to be reminded."

Then, looking right at Griffin, Samantha said, "First stop, Garrett Forester's house."

A tube of paint fell onto the floor. As Samantha's followers stampeded to the checkout, they trampled on the abandoned tube, squirting paint all over Griffin's sneakers that had taken her all summer to design.

"I wish your party is a total bomb!" blurted Griffin aloud. But Samantha had already sashayed to the cash register. *Oh, my gosh! What have I just wished!* thought Griffin, eyes bulging. Then she looked down at her favorite sneakers, totally ruined. "Come on, Libbs. Let's go. My grandma has some awesome paints we can use."

Griffin could hardly contain her anger as they walked the seven blocks to her grandma's house. She clenched her teeth the entire way there.

"Griff, who cares? Who'd want to go to their stupid party anyway?" said Libby.

"It's not that. It's the way Samantha tries to make people feel bad and rubs it in their faces about her party."

"Did you see Samantha's skin, Griff? It's really looking lizardlike. I think her friends are afraid to tell her, but it's getting worse."

"Really?" Griffin smiled. Then she gulped. The witches' chant rang in her head, *In the cauldron boil and bake . . . Lizard's leg and owlet's wing . . .* She wondered, *Did I cast a wish of powerful trouble?*

That wish had been an accident. But what had she wished now—that Samantha's party would be a total bomb? What did that even mean? Griffin felt sick to her stomach.

Libby pressed the doorbell. Classical music trilled. Libby smiled. "I even love your grandma's doorbell!"

"Yeah," said Griffin, still in a terrible mood, though she knew it was hard to stay angry when at her grandma's house. Crystal candy jars jammed with jelly beans rested on tables for visitors. Fresh flowers, including blooming orchids, stretched in every room in every color all year round. Grandma called her flowers "A sunrise in a vase!" It was impossible to sit in a chair without sinking into feather cushions. On the couch Grandma's needlepoint pillows were handcrafted with quotes from her favorite artists, like Matisse: "There are always flowers for those who want to see them."

Grandma Penshine, neat and trim in her gray slacks, black ballet flat shoes, and a hand-knit shawl, greeted them at the door. "If it isn't two of my favorite people in the whole world!" Her soft white hair framed her still-pretty face, and her warm brown eyes twinkled like a mischievous teenager's. Besides laugh lines, she had very few wrinkles. At eighty-five years old, Grandma Penshine looked like most sixty-five-year-olds.

"Hi, Grandma," said Griffin.

"Hi, GP," said Libby, calling Grandma Penshine by her nickname.

Grandma Penshine moved to hug them. "You two seem upset. What's the matter? Did something happen?"

"Nothing, Grandma," said Griffin, still furious, clutching the triste bleu paint.

"We only got one tube of paint," said Libby sadly.

"That's okay. I just thought you two might want a dab of a new special color."

"I wished Samantha's birthday would be a total disaster!" said Griffin.

"Griffin, what's the matter?" asked her grandma.

"The most awful girl in the entire school bought all the paint in the store just as Libby and I were picking ours out."

"How insensitive of her," said Grandma Penshine.

"I wished horrible things on her," said Griffin.

"That's not right either, Griff," she said. "Don't stoop to her level. You're better than that."

"I don't care," said Griffin, with an odd feeling in her stomach. "I hate her," she said, and her eyes glowed yellow.

"Griffin! Your eyes!" said Libby.

"They look a bit yellow," said her grandma.

Griffin ran into the bathroom and stared in the mirror. A yellowish glint reflected in her eyes. Slowly she walked back to Libby and her grandma. "I think I'm tired."

"Libby, why don't you start practicing before our lesson?

Your easels are set up on the back porch. It's such a lovely day! Griffin, can you please help me reach some paintbrushes in my guest room closet?"

"Okay," said Griffin, following her grandma down the hall.

"Griffin, whenever I've seen yellow eyes before it's because a person wasn't eating enough fruit or getting enough sweetness in life. What's the matter?"

"Nothing," said Griffin. She and her grandma stared at each other. Then Griffin asked, "Have you ever wished horrible things on people?"

"Well," she started, and then paused. "I can't say that I haven't wanted to when I got boiling mad, but no, I never did. Wishing horrible things, doing horrible things, saying horrible things—it all twists into your face, making it droop with cruel words and then pinching it up tight. Treat yourself with respect and ignore people who don't treat you with dignity," said her grandma.

Griffin's hands shot up to her face, and her cheeks felt warm. Her eyes grew huge.

"What's the matter?" asked her grandma.

Griffin plopped onto the guest bed. Mariah's face came jutting into her mind, wearing a wicked sneer, each wrinkle pulling tighter and tighter into an evil circus clown smile.

"I just remembered a ninety-two-year-old lady with the most creased face I've ever seen," said Griffin. "Do you think people can *steal* wishes?"

Grandma Penshine quieted. Griffin heard the clock tick and the cotton curtains rustle, and she shivered from a cold breeze that shot straight through the bedroom. Both Griffin and her grandma caught the chills.

"Yes, I believe people can steal wishes. Those people—Wish Stealers is what we used to call them back when I was a girl in Topeka—are the worst kind of people in the world."

Griffin's heart beat out of control.

"Wish Stealers are filled with fear. They are the first people to spit on a dream." Grandma Penshine sneezed and moved to grab a tissue. "Wish Stealers make people ashamed for trying, eat up people's courage, and stomp on their enthusiasm. Do you know why? Because they're afraid. Jealous they can't do it themselves. Wish Stealers are afraid to dream."

Flashes of Mariah's face seared into Griffin's head.

"Wishes are a bit like snowflakes: powerful and fragile at the same time," said Grandma Penshine. "They can melt at any minute but are magnificent just the same. They are filled with nature's *most fierce and wild power*. That's what's in a wish, *a fierce and wild power*."

Suddenly Grandma Penshine couldn't stop coughing.

Hacking. Gasping for air. Her fragile chest heaved for breath.

"Grandma!" shouted Griffin.

Her grandma coughed until her chest looked like it might collapse. "Grandma!" shrieked Griffin, and she ran to grab a glass of water.

✳ ✳ ✳

Nothing happens unless first a dream.

—Carl Sandburg

Chapter

18

First thing Monday morning Griffin slumped down the school hallway. Shadows and bags hung under her eyes. All weekend she'd worried about her grandma. Her coughing attack had been so severe she'd had to lie down and cancel their lesson. *I wish for Grandma Penshine to get well soon* rattled through Griffin's head. Right before school, she slipped the "change the world" penny into her shoe. She figured so much in her world needed changing. Including herself.

"Griffin, did you hear?" said Libby, running up to her.

"Hear what?"

"At Samantha's party! Her dad bought paintball guns as

a surprise so everyone could play in their huge backyard, but the paint cartridges overheated and exploded—a giant paint bomb splattered everywhere!"

Every hair on Griffin's arms stood up. "Really?" she said, bug-eyed. *Did I wish that?* she thought. *A paint bomb!*

"Hey, Griffin! Hi, Libby," said Garrett, coming up to them.

"Hi, Garrett," said Griffin.

"How was Samantha's party? Did you go?" said Libby.

"Yeah, she and some girls came to my house and practically dragged me to the party. Then her parents freaked when paintballs exploded and grafittied their lawn furniture. All the food was ruined and everyone just went home covered in paint. I had to take, like, three showers to get the paint off."

Griffin stared.

"Wow!" said Libby.

Griffin's heart plummeted. Had her wish caused the paint to explode on all the kids? Were tendrils of darkness overtaking her, winding their way around her soul as she stood there? *I need to work faster, try harder, and return these wishes,* she thought.

"Griffin?" said Libby and Garrett at the same time. Her face had turned white.

"Yeah, sorry. I spaced," she said.

"Bye. See you at lunch," Libby said, running off.

"Bye," she said. "Garrett, do you still want to do our project on alchemy and the Pennies for the Planet fund-raiser I texted you about?"

"Yeah," he said.

"We have to ask Mr. Blackwell at lunch. He's the science coordinator and has to give final approval for all the projects at science night."

"Okay," he said.

"Meet you in the teacher's section of the cafeteria," she said.

"Cool," he said, walking off.

Griffin did not notice Samantha in a velvet minidress and knee-high crisscross fur boots lurking by the lockers. "Lunch date?" snarled Samantha.

"It's for the science project, Samantha," said Griffin, willing herself not to wish anything bad on her.

"The one you're going to bomb?" taunted Samantha.

Griffin thought of her grandma. "Our project is gonna rock," said Griffin, and she walked away.

At the start of lunch period Garrett, eating a bag of Fritos, was hovering by the water fountain. "Hey," he said.

"Hi," said Griffin.

"Fritos really make you thirsty," he said. "You want some? They're way better than school lunch!"

Griffin smiled. "No, thanks."

Garrett crunched harder.

Walking over to the teachers' table, Garrett wiped his greasy Fritos hands on his pants. He smelled like a giant corn chip.

"Excuse me, Mr. Blackwell?" said Griffin.

Mr. Blackwell turned to face them. Gooey crumbs stuck to his mustache. "Yes? Is this important enough to disturb my lunch?"

"Sorry to interrupt," said Griffin, "but Mr. Luckner said we had to get your approval for our science night project. We wanted to do our report on the alchemists and their contributions to modern-day science. We also wanted to do a fundraiser that would turn pennies into gold—kinda like the alchemists. A charity called Pennies for the Planet helps kids collect tons of pennies and uses them to stop the destruction of the Amazon rain forest."

Still chewing his food, Mr. Blackwell looked at them. "Do you two really think *pennies* will help save the Amazon rain forest? It's not worth your effort."

Suddenly Griffin felt the "change the world" penny in

her shoe start to burn. "We thought we'd try," she said.

"Actually, my rock band volunteered to play at science night as free entertainment to try to get donations for the planet."

"Really?" said Griffin, looking at Garrett.

"Yeah, my band is awesome. We could totally raise money!"

Food dribbled on Mr. Blackwell's tie. "I had a band once. Every kid thinks he can be in a band. But ninety-nine percent of bands fail. No one shows up to rehearse. Everyone wants it his own way. How long have you had this band of yours, Mr. Forester?"

"Since last summer," said Garrett.

"You'll see."

Griffin reached for her shoe. The sole of her foot was on fire. She took out the labeled penny, and it burned her palm. "Actually, Garrett's band is amazing. They're really talented," she said, even though she had never heard them. "Plus, we already have our first donation: a lucky penny that is worth much more than one cent." She held out her palm, revealing a coin that shot light like a laser.

Mr. Blackwell read the label stuck on the penny, and said, "A little penny to *change the world*. How sweet. Are you two *numismatists* now?"

"What?" said Garrett and Griffin at the same time.

"A new-miss-ma-tist, kiddos. A coin collector of rare and special coins. Look at that! An 1872 Indian Head penny!" His eyebrows scrunched together.

The coin was on fire, shining streaks of light on the cafeteria ceiling.

Walking toward the table, Mr. Reasoner, the metalworks teacher, said, "What is that beautiful radiance? Flash anything shiny at a fish or a metalworks teacher, and both will get lured right in!"

He stooped over and examined the penny in Griffin's hand. "I know an awful lot about coins. Any kind of metal is my specialty. A 1872 Indian Head penny! What a lovely label." Mr. Reasoner sighed and said, "I certainly do wish we could change the world!"

"What's so great about an 1872 Indian Head penny?" asked Garrett.

"Most old pennies aren't worth much, usually one cent or maybe a few dollars. If you're *really* fortunate, every once in a while, you might find an old penny worth ten dollars. If a penny is unpolished and hasn't been touched for hundreds of years, it can actually be worth thousands of dollars, but this penny is probably worth about a hundred and fifty dollars."

"A hundred and fifty dollars!" said Mr. Blackwell, Garrett, and Griffin in unison.

"That's a great start for our fund-raiser!" said Griffin.

"Maybe you'd like me to keep it safe for you?" said Mr. Blackwell. He reached to scoop the penny out of Griffin's hand, but his fingers accidently flicked it instead. A burst of copper shot though the air and landed in the custodian's dirty mop bucket nearby.

SPLASH! sang out, and the penny sank to the bottom of the dark swirling pail. Water swooshed up at the custodian, Mr. Newoski. "Was that a rocket? I was almost blinded!" said the janitor, wiping his eyes.

Garrett and Griffin rushed toward Mr. Newoski. "Are you okay?"

"Yup. I didn't know I'd have to watch for missiles while I mopped!"

Mr. Reasoner and Mr. Blackwell gathered around the container. The mop bucket slopped filthy water everywhere. A sneer seeped out of Mr. Blackwell as he peered into the black bucket. "Well, better get your penny, kids."

Griffin glared at him. "Can we do our project or not?"

"Go right ahead. Let the band play!" He went back to his table. "But don't be disappointed with the results. Being realistic is important."

Mr. Reasoner turned toward the janitor. "Mr. Newoski, there is a valuable penny in this bucket. Do you think we can dump the water so that the kids can get back their coin?"

"Not a problem," he said, plunging his hand straight into the bucket. After fishing on the bottom for the penny for a few seconds, he grabbed it and wiped it dry on his rag. "Little dirt never hurt anybody!" He placed the penny in Griffin's hand. It was now even more spectacular, immaculately clean from the detergent.

"Come by the metal shop at afternoon recess, Griffin," said Mr. Reasoner. "I can give you an empty ring box to keep your penny in."

"Thanks, Mr. Reasoner," she said as she tucked the penny into her pocket.

Garrett and Griffin walked back to the kids' side of the cafeteria. Griffin said, "So you'll play at science night?"

"Yeah. We're great. We're rehearsing tomorrow in my garage. You wanna hear us? Bring your bass so I can hear it. I'm gonna tell the guys we should rename our band the Alchemists."

"What's your band's name now?"

"Five Cool Guys," he said.

She laughed. "I thought we could work on our project tomorrow."

"We already worked on it Friday," said Garrett.

"Yeah, *once*. We have so much more to do," reminded Griffin.

"Fine," said Garrett. "Come to my house tomorrow and see my band, and we'll work after. I'll talk to my friends about the rock concert."

"What rock concert?" she said.

"For the planet," he said.

"Oh, yeah, cool," said Griffin. She hoped his band was good.

At the start of recess Griffin headed to Mr. Reasoner's huge metal shop.

"Hello. Come in, Griffin," he said. "I have this box that will be perfect for your penny. What's this I hear about a fund-raiser?"

"It's for science night. We're collecting pennies for Pennies for the Planet to help save the Amazon rain forest," she said.

"Count me in. I have two huge mayonnaise jars of pennies that I've been waiting to donate to a good cause."

A boy with a goofy grin, reddish hair parted down the middle, and a sprinkling of freckles all over his face was working in the back of the metal shop. He listened to every word. Griffin noticed him eavesdropping but didn't think anything of it.

*   *   *

Keep away from people who try to belittle your ambitions. Small people always do that, but the really great make you feel that you, too, can become great.
—Mark Twain

Chapter 19

At afternoon recess Garrett ran up to Griffin in the yard where she stood in line for basketball shots. "Hey, Griffin," said Garrett, "you'll never believe the stuff I read on the Internet during computer class. These alchemists were so cool! Basil Valentine, Zosimos, and Nicolas Flamel. They all turned lead into gold!"

"That's awesome! I wonder where all that gold went," said Griffin.

"They probably buried it or something," said Garrett.

"Probably." Griffin felt the first raindrop plop onto her head. "Uh-oh. It's gonna pour any second," she said, scanning the gray sky. "Hey, Garrett, I brought you something."

Griffin reached into her pocket for a penny. The previous period she'd rummaged through her backpack, peeked inside Mariah's black case, and studied the remaining pennies. She'd pulled out a penny for Garrett and jammed it in her pocket.

"Really? What?" he said, facing her.

Griffin dug into her pocket, pulled out the coin, and held out her palm.

"I found a few lucky pennies at a shop." She didn't want to tell him much more.

He took it from her, and a few more raindrops drizzled on their heads.

"WATCH OUT!" A spinning rubber ball bounced into a puddle, squirting water all over them.

"Sorry!" called the players.

Garrett's eyes narrowed. "This penny says 'a dad'! Why would I want this stupid penny, Griffin? I never want to see my dad!"

Hail began pelting the kids on the playground. Mrs. Gideon yelled, "Come inside, everybody! Come inside. 'Fair is foul, and foul is fair: / Hover through the fog and filthy air!'" Hoards of kids raced indoors. Griffin didn't know if it was rain or a teardrop in Garrett's eye, but before she could look again, Garrett hurled the penny out of his hand like a hockey puck and yelled, "Like I wish for a dad!" There was a brilliant streak as a disc of shining light skimmed across the wet asphalt and disappeared into the overflowing gutter. Staring at Garrett, Griffin knew he'd seen that strange light too, but before she could speak, he tore through the yard and stomped in a puddle, splashing water all over her.

* * *

Wishes travel in strange ways.

Chapter 20

✳ ✳
✳

Doorbell!" called Griffin's mom from the laundry room in the basement. "Can you see who it is?"

"Sure," said Griffin. She had just texted Garrett after dinner:

Hi. I'm really sorry 4 giving u the penny. Do u still want me 2 come over tom. and see ur band after school?

He texted back:

OK. Can u bring ur bass guitar?

✳ ✳ ✳

She texted:

OK, but I can only stay a ½ hr then my mom wants to pick us up and drive us to the library to work.

He texted:

OK.

Relieved that Garrett was not mad at her, she put her phone down. Eight fifteen p.m. Her dad was working late, and she couldn't imagine who would ring their doorbell. Peeking through the peephole, Griffin saw a man wrapped in a dark coat. Shivers shot through her. "Mom, it's Mr. Schmidt!" called Griffin.

"I'll be right up. Let him in," she called.

Cautiously Griffin opened the door. Mr. Schmidt never came over. *Did Mariah tell him about the pennies before she died?* she wondered.

"Hi, Mr. Schmidt," said Griffin. The eerie night hovered outside, casting long shadows behind him.

"Good evening, Griffin. Sorry to come by so late, but there was something I needed to bring over."

Just then Dr. Penshine came up from the basement. "Hi,

Mike. Please come in. We were so sorry to hear about your great-aunt."

"Thank you," he said, but he did not look at Dr. Penshine. Instead he stared at Griffin. "Actually, I stopped over because of Mariah."

Griffin's throat went dry.

"Although my aunt only met you once, Griffin, she must have been quite taken with you. Maybe you reminded her of herself when she was young. She had long red hair as a girl too."

Griffin cringed.

"Mariah never married or had children, but when I was going through her things in my guest room, I found this box that she left for Griffin. I guess the very afternoon my aunt met her, she wrote this letter. It was taped to it."

Mr. Schmidt read Mariah's note aloud.

Dear Mike,

Please be sure to give this box to that sweet young girl, Griffin Penshine, whom we met at your shop. I have some old memorabilia, not worth anything really, but which may be fun for a young girl!

Mariah W. S.

Mr. Schmidt held out Mariah's box, which had a golden lock on it. Mariah W.S. Did her initials stand for Weatherby Schmidt or *Wish Stealer*? The golden key. Now it made sense. Griffin stared at the menacing gift, afraid of what was inside. More stolen wishes? Hideous, horrible things? Things Mariah had bought with people's wishes?

"Well, Griff. It's flattering that you met Mariah only once and she remembered you like this," said her mom.

"Mariah was meticulous—a memory like a steel trap. Never forgot anything or anybody," said Mr. Schmidt. "Always kept wonderful records."

Griffin still did not come forward. "Griff, what's the matter?" asked her mom.

"Well, it has a lock on it," Griffin said, and gulped, hoping Mr. Schmidt would take it away.

"That's easy. Any pair of pliers could take it off. I couldn't find the key, and I didn't want to damage it before giving it to you as my aunt wished."

Griffin's stomach twisted into knots.

"Would you like me to cut the lock for you?" he said.

Griffin leapt forward. "No. It's okay. I, uh, like surprises." She snatched the box from him. What if it was something that could hurt her mom if she saw it. The box was heavy. Her face drained to white again.

"Thanks," said Griffin.

"Thank *you*," he said. "I better get going. Good night."

Griffin spied through the peephole as Mr. Schmidt disappeared into the darkness.

"Do you want to open the box and see what she left you?" asked her mom.

"I think I'll wait," said Griffin. She didn't want her mom involved with the wishes. *What if the contents of the box are wicked?* she wondered.

"If that isn't discipline!" said her mom, laughing.

Griffin put the box down and hugged her mom tightly, hugged her maybe even for protection. Then she heaved the box up the stairs to her bedroom.

Griffin lay on her bed, staring at the box. "Hi, Charlemagne," Griffin whispered as she picked him up from his upstairs terrarium. He crawled toward her on the bed. "I guess I should open it. It can't get much worse, right?" Griffin got up, locked her door, and moved to pull down her bedroom shades. Through the window she peered out at the murky night. She could see the top of Mr. Schmidt's house. Lights were on in his attic. She yanked down the shade and knelt before her bed. Heart racing, hands trembling, she took the golden key out from the side pocket of her backpack where she'd left it, and put it in the keyhole.

The box top sprang open. Charlemagne shot his head inside his shell so quickly, he lost his balance and almost toppled off the bed. Gently Griffin picked him up, placed him by her side, and peered into the box. Inside were four things: a Topeka Inn guest book register with a cracked leather cover, a large bloodred garnet ring, a skein of old gray yarn, and the black obsidian disc from Mr. Schmidt's shop with the card that read *Obsidian mirror—used by the ancient alchemists, passed down from Aztec priests. See your future!*

Griffin inhaled ancient dust from the leather book and its mildewing pages.

The old yarn smelled stale and musty. It looked like a coiled spiderweb. She didn't want to touch it. As bright as molten lava, the ring flashed red light all over her ceiling. She averted her eyes. The shiny black stone disc reflected only darkness. The guest book gazed up at her with a helpless, lost look. Picking it up, she blew dust off the cover and opened the first faded page.

✳   ✳   ✳

Best wishes.

Chapter 21

✳ ✳
✳

Griffin's eyes raced up and down the first page of the guest book. Three different columns listed the names of guests, the dates they stayed at the inn, and their room numbers. Some names were funny. Some were old-fashioned. Ethel, Mabel, and Selma stayed in room 9. Mr. Leroy Simmons and Annabelle Lee Simmons stayed in room 8. Penciled next to some of the names were tiny words, hardly legible. Griffin zoomed in on the pencil scratches. Next to Annabelle Lee Simmons's name were the words "best friend." Next to Selma's name was "a husband." To the left of Hatter Bloom's name was "money." Besides Georgina Pironi's name read "go home to Italy."

Did Mariah write down the wishes she stole from these guests? wondered Griffin.

Scanning each and every column, Griffin looked for a penciled word that would match even one of the eleven pennies she had under her bed. Suddenly her finger stopped dead next to Florence L. Daniellson: "puppy." *Puppy.* "PUPPY!" screamed Griffin.

Furiously flipping through the rest of the pages, Griffin searched for more matches, but there were no others. "PUPPY!" she yelled again.

"Griffin? Are you okay!" called her mom through the door. "What are you shouting about?"

After slipping the guest book and Mariah's box under her bed, Griffin opened her bedroom door. "Hi," said Griffin.

"Did I hear you say, 'puppy'?" Her mom sat down on her bed. "Why are you talking about a puppy?"

"No reason," she said.

"No reason? Do you want a puppy because the baby is coming and you feel left out?"

"Mom, I can't wait to meet the baby! I just had an idea about a puppy for a project. That's all," Griffin said while crossing her fingers. Charlemagne crawled on Griffin's lap. "Plus, I don't know if Charlemagne would feel too safe with a puppy. A puppy might think Charlemagne's a football."

Charlemagne ducked his head inside his shell again. Dr. Penshine rubbed Charlemagne's belly.

"Have you decided what you and Dad are going to name the baby?" asked Griffin, wanting to change the subject.

"Why don't we go up to the roof and I'll tell you."

Griffin's mom had installed a mini-observatory on their roof years ago. Three telescopes stood ready during the spring, summer, and fall. The roof looked like any ordinary roof from the front, but on the back her mom had built a platform for stargazing. Dr. Penshine had named her three telescopes Galileo, Sir Isaac, and Copernicus. Griffin's mom knew all eighty-eight constellations in the sky.

Together they walked to the rooftop. The cool breeze brushed against Griffin's cheeks. She was relieved they couldn't see Mr. Schmidt's house and its creepy shadows from the roof. Thankfully the platform faced only their backyard and the deep night sky beyond it.

"Here, Griff, look through that telescope and tell me what you see."

Griffin looked through the telescope and saw Polaris, the planet Jupiter, the constellation Sagittarius, and the swirling spiral galaxies M81 and M82.

"I see stars that must be millions of light-years away," said Griffin.

"In one of those distant and deep parts of space is a hidden and beautiful constellation called Caelum. It can only be seen at the equator or in the southern hemisphere, where your dad and I gazed at it on our honeymoon. We want to name the new baby Caelum if he's a boy and Caela is she's a girl."

"What does Caelum mean?" asked Griffin.

"It's a constellation named in 1754 by my favorite astronomer, Lacaille. Caelum means 'the heavens.' Its second meaning is '*les burins*,' which is an old instrument for engraving on copper."

"Engraving on copper? Like a penny!" said Griffin.

"A *burin* probably helped engrave the models for the first pennies."

"Wow!" said Griffin as she drank up the night sky filled with millions of bright stars. I can't wait to meet Caelum or Caela!" Then she had an idea. "Mom, wait here!"

Griffin ran downstairs and lunged under her bed. She took the label off the "baby" penny so her mom wouldn't become suspicious. Bounding back up the stairs, Griffin held out the penny to her mother. It glowed wildly under the canopy of stars. "This is a lucky penny I found."

"Really?" said her mom.

"Yeah," said Griffin. "Do you want to make a wish about the baby?" she asked.

"Okay," said her mom, smiling. She put the penny in her left palm, closing her fingers tightly around it. In her right hand she held Griffin's hand.

A meteor whizzed by overhead.

"A shooting star!" exclaimed Griffin. At that exact moment her mother made a wish and gently placed the penny down on the railing.

The door to the roof swung open. "Hello, everybody. What are you doing up here?" asked Griffin's dad.

"Hi, Dad! Mom and I just saw a shooting star!" said Griffin.

"You know what Mom says about shooting stars, right?"

"They're lucky!" said Griffin, feeling better for the first time in a while.

"Griffin gave me a lucky penny to make a wish for the baby," said her mom to her dad. Then Dr. Penshine scooped the penny off the railing. It was wet, now covered in dew. It sparkled even more like a star that had landed.

"Mom, we need to save this and give it to the baby when she or he is born."

"Good idea. Where should we keep it?" asked Dr. Penshine.

"I know," said Griffin, taking the penny from her mom. "Good night!"

"Good night, Griff," called her parents, smiling.

Griffin raced downstairs, but before turning into her own bedroom, she tiptoed into the guest room that had been converted into a nursery. The penny felt warm in her palm. Very carefully she placed the penny in a keepsake box on a high shelf next to the crib. The "baby" penny glowed.

✳   ✳   ✳

Starlight, star bright,
first star I see tonight.
I wish I may, I wish I might,
have the wish I wish tonight.

Chapter

22

L ouder!" shouted Garrett over the cacophony of banging drums inside his garage. Griffin forced a smile. Her mom had dropped her off after school and had gone to run an errand. "In thirty minutes I'll be back to pick you both up," she'd said.

"Louder, guys!" Garrett yelled again as he pounded on his drums.

Covering her ears was what Griffin really wanted to do. She had a splitting headache from thinking about Mariah's gifts. *What did Mariah use that creepy yarn for? Why did she have that bloodred ring?* Mariah's antique black mirror gave Griffin the chills. Did it reflect only the dark side of things?

Did it show the sadness people felt when their stolen wishes never came true? The song ended, but no one finished at the same time.

"Hey, Griffin," called Jason Scott. "Garrett wants our band to play for science night. We usually charge for our gigs, but because this is Garrett's science project, we're going to play for free."

"Thanks," said Griffin, swallowing the lump in her throat.

"What do you think, Griffin?" asked Garrett as he stepped out of the open garage onto the driveway, where Griffin stood. Griffin didn't know what to say.

"Cool." She gulped. "It's really nice your mom lets you have the garage to practice in."

"It's mostly our hangout. We just practice here when we feel like it," said Garrett.

"Oh," said Griffin.

Garrett looked at Griffin funny. "Hey, where's your bass? Did you bring it?" he asked.

Griffin was so afraid that she wouldn't be able to play because of the curse that she hadn't brought her bass guitar. "I totally forgot it, but I have some video of me playing bass this summer. I was in a band at the music conservatory where I take lessons."

"Cool," said the guys, passing around Griffin's phone and watching her play her bass guitar.

"You're amazing!" said Todd Wherry, who played electric keyboard.

"Cool stuff," said Ethan Bergwein, the lead singer.

"Thanks," said Griffin. Inside she shrank. *Maybe I'm not a good player anymore because of the curse. I wish to become an amazing bass guitarist* sirened through her head.

"Hey, guys. Let's break for today," Garrett called.

Griffin looked at her watch. They had five minutes until her mom picked them up.

"We've been jamming hard. Let's meet the same time next Tuesday. I gotta go work on that stupid science project."

All the guys started high-fiving one another. Two of the boys besides Garrett went to their school: the lead singer, Ethan, and the guitar player, Jason, who Griffin recognized from classes at Dadesville's music center. Todd Wherry and Kurt Keene, who were packing their instruments, went to the rival middle school.

"Mom! We're done!" screamed Garrett to the dark upstairs windows.

Nothing happened.

"She must be asleep." Garrett shrugged.

Jason's older brother, whose car was at the end of the

driveway, blasted the horn. "Come on, kiddies, jump in the Batmobile!" he yelled. The four boys lugged their instruments down the driveway.

"Later," they called.

"Later," said Garrett, banging some final beats and fills on his drums. "I'm just gonna put some of these speakers away."

"Okay," said Griffin, who sat down at a broken piano in the front of the garage.

"Do you think my band is bad?" Garrett said.

"No," she said, not meeting his eyes.

"Come on, tell me the truth. You think my band stinks, don't you?" said Garrett.

"No, I think you guys could be amazing—"

"Could be? Like we're *not* or something?" he said, sounding defensive.

"No, I didn't mean it like that—"

"You sound like Mr. Blackwell," he said with a sharp tone.

"No, I don't! He's a Wish Stealer!" Griffin blurted out.

"A what?" said Garrett, staring at her.

"He just makes fun of people for trying," said Griffin.

"Whatever," said Garrett, turning away from her. He beat loudly on his drum.

"What's going on in here?" asked Garrett's mom,

sticking her head into the garage. She looked very tired.

"Nothing," said Garrett.

"Hi. You must be Griffin," said Garrett's mom.

"Hi, Mrs. Forester," Griffin said, standing up from the piano bench to shake her hand. "Nice to meet you."

"Were you about to play the piano?" she asked.

"No. I play bass guitar," she said.

Mrs. Forester had the same dancing, kind blue eyes as Garrett.

"Mom, my band's going to play a concert for science night."

"I'll make sure to get out of work early so that I can be there."

"But Griffin said my band stinks. I don't go to the music center like *she* does."

Griffin's mouth flew open. "Garrett! I didn't say that!"

"I would love to send you to the music center, Garrett." The saddest sigh deflated out of Mrs. Forester. "We just can't afford it right now. I better let you kids do your work. Nice to meet you, Griffin." She headed inside.

Just then Dr. Penshine honked the car horn. Griffin swiveled her head toward the car and then back to Garrett.

"I don't feel like working on our project tonight," said Garrett angrily.

"I have more stuff to do on my part," said Griffin, her eyes now moist. "I guess I'll just work on that."

"Yeah," he said, not looking at her.

"Bye, Garrett," she said.

But Garrett had already bolted inside his house and slammed the door.

✳ ✳ ✳

People's dreams are fragile—be gentle.

Chapter

23

Griffin slid into the passenger seat of her mom's car. "How'd it go?" asked her mom.

"Fine," said Griffin, staring out the window.

"How's his band?" asked her mom.

"Fine," she said unconvincingly.

"So they weren't very good?"

"I don't know." She shrugged.

"I see," said Griffin's mom. "Where's Garrett? Is he coming with us?"

"He's not coming," said Griffin.

"Why not?" she said.

"Garrett's mad at me. Garrett's mom said they couldn't

afford to send Garrett to the music center for lessons, he thinks I think his band stinks, and now he doesn't want to come to the library," said Griffin in a single breath. "I really am a Wish Stealer." She bit down on her trembling lip.

"What's a *Wish Stealer*?"

"Someone who makes people afraid to try. That's what Grandma told me."

"I see," said her mom as she backed the car out of the driveway. "I have to agree with Grandma. Wish Stealers are awful, the worst kind of people."

Griffin stared at her mom. Tears filled her eyes. *Does my own mom think I'm awful?*

The car stopped at the stop sign at the end of Garrett's street. "But you are far from a Wish Stealer."

Griffin couldn't look her mom in the eyes. How little her mom knew.

A group of pigeons congested the road, and the car slowed again. "Remember when we saw that beautiful duck on Fern Lake?" asked her mom.

"Yes," said Griffin as she watched the pigeons flap to the curb.

"It seems like a duck is just gliding along like magic. But do you know that underwater it's kicking and paddling, moving its little webbed feet so fast, working hard to move through that water?"

"Yeah," said Griffin.

"I think that's how wishes work. Like when astronauts walked on the moon, someone made a wish and dared to dream something impossible at the time. But then someone dared to work for the wish. I'm sorry Garrett is sensitive about his band right now, but with a little practice I bet they could be great."

Griffin stared out the window.

"What timing!" said Dr. Penshine, and she pulled into the ice cream store's parking lot and got the best parking spot.

"Mom, what are we doing?" asked Griffin.

"The very first way to approach a problem is to relax and get a scoop of rocky road ice cream!" said her mom, laughing.

"What?" said Griffin, laughing too.

"I just remembered I got an e-mail that the music center is holding open auditions for reduced rates for really good students. I can forward the e-mail to Garrett's mom if you like. I have her e-mail from the school directory."

"Okay," said Griffin.

"There are always a couple ways to solve a problem."

Griffin laughed. "Mom, after our ice cream cones, can you drop me off at the library?"

"Sure. How about I pick you up in an hour? Is that enough time?"

"Thanks, " said Griffin. Her mom's words ran through Griffin's mind. *There are always a couple ways to solve a problem.* But the new idea she had just might get her into big trouble.

* * *

Even magic has a secret.

Chapter
24

✳ ✳
✳

Fingers steady on the keyboard, Griffin typed in her new password, WISH.

Kids were allowed thirty minutes on library computers for research. Griffin clicked on Google. She ripped a scrap of paper out of her notebook. Two names were written on it:

Florence L. Daniellson: puppy.
Garrett Forester: a dad.

She entered the first name. Florence L. Daniellson, Topeka, Kansas.

A recent obituary popped up:

August 4
Busby, Elmer Bingham. Ninety-two, Topeka,
Kansas. Survivors: Wife: Florence L. Daniellson
Busby. Children: Lorraine, Henry, and Paul.
Grandchildren: Lucy and Roger. Funeral home
address . . .

Could this be the same Florence L. Daniellson who'd
wished for a puppy long ago? August 4 was only a few weeks
ago. There was a good chance that Florence L. Daniellson
Busby was still alive . . . and about the right age for a wish if
she were close to her husband's age. Griffin copied down the
funeral home address.

Next she typed in the words "Forester, Alaska, fisherman."
An Alaskan newspaper came up: the *Nome Nugget*, the oldest
Alaskan newspaper. Griffin clicked on the link. The article
was titled BIG FISH! A grainy picture of a man standing proudly
next to a giant fish filled the screen. Under the picture a cap-
tion read:

Brian Patterson Forester, of Nome, Alaska,
catches a 59 lb. 52 inch king salmon! Looks like

this former landlubber from Topeka, Kansas, has really learned to fish in the rough waters of Alaska! Brian said he is dedicating this catch to his son, Garrett.

Griffin looked up the address for the *Nome Nugget* and wrote that down too.

"Griffin!" someone called.

Rotating her seat, she spotted Garrett walking toward her. Quickly she closed her notebook and the window on the computer screen. "Garrett! What are you doing here?"

"I wanted to get some more alchemy books, and my mom said she won't let me get a dog if I didn't come," he said.

"Garrett, I'm really sorry if I hurt your feelings about your band. I didn't mean to at all," said Griffin.

He said nothing.

"I didn't know you wanted a dog. That's so cool," said Griffin.

"Whatever," he said. They walked to a long table, sat on opposite ends, and worked on their project in silence. Garrett did not look at Griffin once.

Garrett and Griffin walked outside at five thirty.

Beautiful violin music floated through the dark courtyard in front of the library. "That music is so incredible," said Griffin, spotting the lonely, sad musician again.

"Yeah, I bet he practices a lot," shot Garrett, skimming a rock down the sidewalk.

The large town clock rang, drowning out the musician's Tchaikovsky violin concerto. The man stopped playing, hung his head, and waited for the clock to cease chiming.

Griffin wiggled off her left shoe. Lately she'd been keeping a few pennies in each shoe just in case.

"Not another penny!" said Garrett, watching her.

But Griffin just stared straight ahead at the musician, flipping the penny in her hand. "Excuse me, sir?" called Griffin to the violinist.

The musician looked up, surprised, like no one had ever called him "sir" in his whole life. "Your violin sounds amazing. What's your name?" Griffin asked.

"Stanley," he said.

"I'm Griffin."

"Hi," he said.

He plucked the gloomiest notes on his violin. "Stick to your studies, kids, so you don't end up like me!" This time he played an angry chord. His violin strings screeched in pain as he sawed against them with his bow.

"Stanley, I have a lucky penny for you to wish on," said Griffin, opening her hand.

Stanley stopped his violin and looked at the shiny penny in Griffin's palm. "That is very kind of you," he said, bowing his head. "But I'm gonna need more than a penny after quitting my job and pouring my life savings into a dream!"

"You can't give up," said Griffin. "Here, make a wish. Just try!"

"Not everyone has a perfect life like you, Griffin," said Garrett.

"Believe me, my life is far from perfect," said Griffin sadly.

For the first time Garrett's and Griffin's eyes met. Tears brimmed in Griffin's eyes.

Stanley gently took the penny from her. Taped across it was the word "success."

"Success!" he read, and started to laugh bitterly. "To make a living doing what I love would be the greatest success to me."

Holding the penny tightly, he closed his eyes as if seeing a strange and faraway dream. Then he shouted, "I wish to be a success!" He rocketed the penny high up in the dark sky. Upward it streaked like a fiery comet. At that same instant the night sprinklers burst on. The blazing penny, already in the air, became engulfed in one of the water jets and began dancing. It bobbed gloriously on the shooting water.

Craning their necks, the three of them gasped as the penny pranced high in the air, sparkling light everywhere, like fluorescent fireworks. "Wow!" said Stanley, smiling for the first time. He grabbed his bow and began playing the most beautiful music, the *Paganini Etudes,* to accompany the shooting water.

"Griffin!" yelled her mom from the car window.

Griffin scooped up her backpack. "My mom can drive you home if you want, Garrett."

"No, thanks. I got a ride."

"Okay," said Griffin, trying to make eye contact, but Garrett had already turned his back.

"Bye, Stanley. Good luck," called Griffin.

Stanley bowed and continued playing as the water waltzed.

✳ ✳ ✳

The future belongs to those who
believe in the beauty of their dreams.
—Eleanor Roosevelt

Chapter

25

Bedroom door: locked. Shades: drawn. Griffin tiptoed to her desk and switched on a tiny desk light. The hands of her clock arched toward midnight. Carefully she unfolded the piece of notebook paper.

Florence L. Daniellson: puppy.
Garrett Forester: a dad.

Griffin stared at the paper. She grabbed a pen and began the first sentence.

Dear Mrs. Florence L. Daniellson Busby,

I am very sorry to hear about your husband. I am sending my condolences. I wanted you to know that, by accident, I may have something that once belonged to you. If you wished for a puppy and threw a coin into a fountain in front of the Topeka Inn when you were a girl, please contact me at the address below. If not, please ignore this letter.

Sincerely,

G. Penshine

Griffin stuffed the letter into an envelope and licked the envelope shut. On the outside of the envelope she wrote:

To: The funeral director

Please forward this letter to Mrs. Florence L. Daniellson Busby. Thank you.

From: A well-wisher.

Sticking that envelope inside a bigger envelope, she wrote the address of the funeral home where Florence's husband's funeral had been held. Griffin slumped back into her desk chair. She was trying her best to return these wishes, but she wasn't sure she was doing anything right. Taking another deep breath, she ripped off a second piece of paper. She was more determined than ever to help Garrett. Maybe if she helped him, he would not be mad at her anymore. With her pen poised, she began:

Dear Mr. Brian Patterson Forester,

I'm a friend of your son, Garrett. I Googled you and found out you lived in Nome. I hope I'm writing to the right person. If I am, please write back. There is something I need to tell you. Thank you.

Sincerely,

G. Penshine

* * *

She enclosed this letter in an envelope, sealed it, and wrote on the front:

Please forward mail to MR. Brian Patterson Forester of Nome, Alaska, catcher of the big fish. Thank you.

FROM: G. Penshine.

In very neat cursive letters Griffin wrote the address to the *Nome Nugget*, care of the fishing department, on the outside of the second envelope.

Griffin thought she would mail these letters from the mailbox by the school yard. If her mom found out she was sending letters to strangers, she'd *really* get in trouble. Maybe she shouldn't even sign her name? Maybe she should use a fake address? *Wait a minute!* thought Griffin. Maybe she should use her grandma's address? Griffin decided to use her own address on Florence's letter, and her grandmother's address on Garrett's dad's envelope. Two strange letters coming to her house would be too obvious. The grandfather clock chimed again. Griffin's parents were fast asleep.

She reached under her bed and removed the ring, black mirror, and yarn from Mariah's box. Griffin placed the ring on top of the mirror. *Why did Mariah give these to me?*

"Owwww!" Griffin's hand shot up to cover her eyes from a blaring light. The garnet ring and mirror threw a violent glow onto the ceiling, bathing the whole room a bloody red. Steadying herself, Griffin squinted her eyes and examined the ring again. She picked up the black disc, the strange stone polished like a smooth lake. She gazed into its pools of darkness. Her reflection was distorted. In the blackness she looked like an old lady. *Is that my future? A rotted Wish Stealer like Mariah?* thought Griffin. She flung the black disc under the bed, where it shattered into shards. "Oh, no!" Then she jumped into bed and, tunneling under the covers, she gathered the blankets tight all around her.

✳   ✳   ✳

Hold fast to dreams
For if dreams die
Life is a broken-winged bird
That cannot fly.
—Langston Hughes

Chapter

26

✳   ✳
✳

Griffin lumbered her way through the hallways toward the science room. Today the oral reports on famous scientists were due. Carrying her clumsy poster board made it difficult to walk. The board caught currents in the hallway as if a wind were blowing against her.

"Hi, Libby. Can't wait to see you at my sleepover party on Saturday!" called Samantha as Libby and Griffin walked down the hall. "It's going to be so much fun! Free makeup and my dad's products for all of us."

Griffin could hardly move with all her books and the poster flapping against her body, but she turned in time to look at Samantha. The girls surrounding Samantha shot Griffin nasty looks as she passed them. "Libby?" said Griffin, confused.

"She e-mailed me really late last night. I'll tell you about it later. I'm so not going," she whispered. "I can't believe her parents let her have a party, like, every weekend!"

Griffin's heart whirled. She'd talked to Libby late last night on the phone. Why hadn't Libby told her about Samantha's invitation? Would Libby change her mind and go to Samantha's party?

A new feeling twisted in her stomach.

"Bye, Griff," said Libby as they parted for different hallways. Griffin continued alone to the science room.

"Okay. Let's see how the projects turned out," said Mr. Luckner as kids shuffled into the classroom. "Put your posters on the back counter and then take a seat." Griffin dropped her books onto her desk.

"Hey, Griffin. If I don't finish my stupid science night project, I'm going to fail because of your no homework idea!" said David Hunt.

"You'd fail because you didn't do your project. Don't blame me!" she said.

"Collie Redmond, a report on Albert Einstein," called Mr. Luckner.

"I, uh, was working so hard on science night that I got behind," said Collie.

"No excuses. Next. Harrison Slovis, Sir Isaac Newton. Come on up . . ."

"Mr. Luckner, the science night thing has really—"

"Are you ready to give your report today or not?" boomed Mr. Luckner from the back of the room, where he sat to grade the presentations.

"Nope."

"Next: Griffin Penshine," called Mr. Luckner. "Have you completed your Marie Curie report?"

Griffin stood up. Hard, mean stares sliced through her. The closer the science night deadline, the madder everyone became. "Yes," said Griffin as she walked to the front of the class. David Hunt's and Michael Janis's faces snarled with hostility. Even the skeleton in the back of the room seemed to grin an evil smile. Garrett's desk was empty. *Where was he?* Looking out at the class, Griffin felt nauseous. "Marie Curie was one of the most famous scientists in the world."

"We don't care!" whispered Michael Janis, sitting in the front row.

Griffin cleared her throat and continued. "Marie was born in Poland in 1867, studied in France, and won two Nobel Prizes, in physics and in chemistry."

"Doesn't matter. She's dead!" mumbled David Hunt, also sitting in the front.

Griffin narrowed her eyes at him. "For four years, night and day, she worked in an unheated shed to discover the element radium."

"Nerd!" heckled Michael.

Gritting her teeth, clenching her jaw, and planting her feet on the tiled floor, Griffin said the next few lines of her report staring at Michael and David. "Many people made fun of Marie Curie, told her she was crazy, said she couldn't be a scientist, that she was just a woman, that she was reaching too high. People were cruel, stupid, and mean to her, but Marie Curie never gave up. She never let people's ignorance, jealousy, or fear stop her."

David and Michael stared back.

"Marie Curie said if she ever was lucky enough to find radium, she hoped it would have a beautiful color. When she did finally find it, radium was more than a beautiful color, it had *spontaneous luminosity*, which meant it was bright and glowing like a star. Marie Curie is one of the most respected and famous scientists to ever live."

"Thank you, Griffin," said Mr. Luckner. "I like how you focused on her persistence. Overall, great job. Though I would have liked to hear more about her daily dedication and routine. Nice poster."

Griffin sat in her seat, her face as red as her hair and almost as red as the cardboard Mars whirling over her head.

✳   ✳   ✳

We must have perseverance
and above all confidence in ourselves.
—Marie Curie

Chapter
27

After class Griffin trudged back to her locker. A yellow Post-it note stuck on it read:

NOT INVITED

Griffin flicked the sticker off and jammed it into her backpack. Stacking her books on the cold linoleum floor, she turned her head in time to see that freckled boy who had been working in the back of the metal shop the other day. He passed by her locker, stared, but didn't say a word. Then from the corner of her eye she noticed Kristina headed toward her.

"Hey, Griffin," said Kristina.

"Hi, Kristina," Griffin said sadly. If only someone would give *her* a real lucky penny right then.

"Griffin, I want you to know nothing has happened since I made that wish on the penny you gave me! 'Most beautiful'— what a joke! I tried out for the tap-dancing team, the drill team, and the cheerleading team and messed up in all of them."

"I'm sorry, Kristina."

"You said the penny was lucky, but I just looked really dumb."

"You didn't look dumb, Kristina. You tried."

"I wish I could get that stupid penny back from the water fountain and undo my wish, because I think that penny was unlucky." Kristina's face began turning a blotchy red color. "Actually, I think *you're* unlucky, Griffin!"

Griffin slammed her locker hard. "No, Kristina, I'm not. Maybe your mom was right about you!"

"You're mean!" said Kristina, turning and running down the hall.

Why did I say that? I'm becoming a Wish Stealer! thought Griffin. "Kristina!" called Griffin, but her voice just echoed in the empty hallway.

After school Griffin slunk toward the sidewalk mailbox. Would Libby, her best friend since first grade when they'd both accidently worn matching socks three days in a row, want to become friends with Samantha? Could Samantha bewitch even Libby? Griffin's heart plummeted. Would Samantha convince Libby to go to her party?

A creak let out when Griffin opened the slot and dropped the two letters in. "Good luck," she muttered, and shuffled away, head bowed. Griffin looked at her watch. The first raindrop splattered on her head.

Honk! Honk! sounded from her father's car.

Her dad rolled down his window. "Hurry, Griff. It's going to pour!"

Griffin slid into the passenger seat.

"Hi. A big storm is coming to Dadesville. Weatherman predicts six inches of rain—thunder, lightning, the whole shebang. We have to go to Grandma's house and stock her up with food before your music lesson. She's not feeling so well."

Griffin's insides contorted into a thousand knots. "Do you think Grandma will be okay?" she whispered. She watched as the rain spit arrows onto the windshield.

"She's one strong lady. I think she'll be fine. How was school today?"

"Okay," she mumbled, and thought of the cruel boys in science class as she gave her Marie Curie report.

"Just okay?" he said.

"Yeah, okay." Griffin felt her stomach tighten again. She couldn't flush the image of Mariah out of her head. Her pinched face lurched into Griffin's head so fast that Griffin shot up her hand to hold her forehead.

"Griffin, what's the matter?" said her dad.

"Headache. A *real bad* headache, Dad," whispered Griffin.

* * *

Don't let today's disappointments cast a shadow on tomorrow's dreams.

Chapter

28

A jumble of trumpets, oboes, bassoons, and drums being played, along with the rain pelting outside the music center, sounded like the whole world was coming undone. Griffin's head pounded. She couldn't wait for her bass guitar lesson to be over. Then she could go home and sink into her own bed. Pull the covers over her head. Try to make sense of so many things going wrong.

She walked toward music room 3. Her lesson started in ten minutes. Chiming in unison with the raindrops, the most soothing music rippled down the hall. Griffin followed the heavenly sounds and peeked inside the open auditorium door. A woman with pitch-black hair in a long braid sat onstage playing a golden harp. After trilling the last notes, the woman stopped, bowed her head, and then smiled at Griffin. "Hello," she called.

"You're so good," said Griffin.

"Thanks from me and my golden harp. Would you like to see it?"

"Sure," said Griffin, walking up onto the stage.

"I'm Aurora," said the lady, holding out her hand.

"I'm Griffin. How long have you played?"

"Since I was a little girl. I'm on a national tour giving concerts, but when we pulled into Kansas, I had to see my old music teacher on the way through Dadesville."

"Wow!" The harp was as tall as Griffin. "This must be hard to move."

"Nothing that can't be done if you just go slow and be careful," said Aurora, smiling.

"Yeah," said Griffin, transfixed on Aurora's aquamarine eyes. They looked like crystals.

"Griffin Penshine, next!" called her bass guitar teacher's voice from the hallway.

"I gotta go," said Griffin. "Bye, Aurora." She walked off the stage back toward her lesson in room 3. She wondered what she would do if Florence and Garrett's dad wrote her back.

Griffin's fingers felt numb on the four stainless steel strings of her bass guitar. Over and over again she fumbled her scales. Her left hand plucked, but her fingers cramped, and none of the sounds blended. Her teacher exhaled a long, frustrated breath.

Griffin clutched the neck and fret board of her guitar with her right hand, but her palm was so sweaty that the soft cushions of her fingers slipped over the strings and messed up the walking bass line.

"Griffin," said Mr. Castanara. He removed his glasses and stared at her. "Have you practiced?"

"No, I . . ." *I wish to become an amazing bass guitarist* rang in her head like a sad joke.

"Please stay here by yourself and use this time to practice."

"Okay," said Griffin, staring at the four steel strings. She was afraid if she looked up she might cry.

Mr. Castanara left the room, but kept the door ajar. Griffin's eyes clouded over with tears.

"Griffin? Is that you?" It was Jason Scott, thrusting his head into the room, carrying his guitar.

"Hi," she said, sucking in her breath trying to stop any tears from falling.

"What are you doing here?" he asked.

"My teacher wanted me to work on some scales."

"I just wanted to say *thanks a lot* for saying our band stinks!" he said.

"What do you mean?" she asked. Her heart began to drum.

"Garrett wasn't in school today," he said.

"Yeah," she answered.

"Do you know why?"

"Why?" Her back tightened.

"'Cause he said you said our band *stinks*! He skipped school to stay home all day to solo practice his drums."

"WHAT?" said Griffin. "I never said that!"

"*We* aren't the ones who stink!" he said.

The aroma of hot chicken soup tantalized Griffin as she trudged through the front door. "Nothing better than soup on a cold, wet night!" said her mom.

Griffin slumped right past the kitchen.

"Hey," called her mom. "Best bowl of soup in Kansas! Grandma's own recipe."

All Griffin wanted to do was cry into her pillow. But the soup smelled so good.

"Hot bowl ready for you, Griff."

"Okay," said Griffin, pulling off her boots and raincoat. She walked into the kitchen.

"Hi," said her mom, studying her face. "You look tired."

"Yeah," said Griffin, taking a seat. She dragged her spoon through the clear broth. Bobbing in the liquid were celery floats and carrot cushions.

"So how'd your lesson go?" asked her mom.

"Not so great," she said. "I haven't really practiced. I've had a lot of schoolwork."

"It's been a busy week for you. It happens to all of us. How'd your Marie Curie report go in school today?"

"Fine," said Griffin. "Mom, I think I'm getting sick. Can I stay home from school tomorrow?"

Her mom spun around. "Hmm," she said, feeling Griffin's forehead with her palm. "You don't feel hot at all. Eat your soup. You could be coming down with something. Let's see how you feel in a little bit, okay? Oh, and Libby called."

Maybe she's decided to go to Samantha's party after all, thought Griffin.

"Do you want to see an amazing constellation with my telescope? Now that the rain has stopped, the sky is oddly bright."

"Which constellation?"

"Draco is lit up tonight, brighter than I've seen him in a long time."

"Who's Draco?"

"The dragon, remember?"

How could I forget the dragon? she thought. The whole world was bursting with wicked dragons . . . the kids in her science class, Kristina, Jason at the music center. Was she even losing Libby, too?

"Do you want to take a look?" asked her mom.

Holding her bowl up to her mouth, Griffin slurped her soup to consume the final golden droplets. "Sure."

They climbed the stairs. On the roof, adjusting the telescope, her mom said, "There he is! The dragon. Ancient Greeks believed dragons were the guardians of temples and treasures."

Griffin looked through the telescope, scanning the five stars that composed the constellation. The flickering stars hurt her eyes, so she turned the telescope away from her.

"What? What is it, Griff?"

"Nothing. My eyes hurt from squinting."

"Did you see something?" asked her mom, and she took another look. "It's just Draco waiting." Reaching out her palm, Dr. Penshine felt Griffin's head again. "You know, you are warm. Why don't you go to sleep."

"Good night, Mom," said Griffin, and she walked down the stairs to her bedroom. Diving into bed with her clothes on, she sunk into a deep sleep—dreaming of dragons with the faces of the kids at school.

✳   ✳   ✳

Dragons guard the temples
of transformation.

Chapter

29

For the first time in her life Griffin dreaded going to school. Dreaded what horrible thing might happen next. She had hoped for a high fever, hoped she'd wake up hacking. But when she woke up, her mom was already by her bed feeling her forehead. "Your temperature is just fine. Are you feeling better?"

Griffin took a deep breath. She did feel fine, just not in her heart. It was stuck in a sunk position. "Yeah, I'll be okay," she said, sighing as she got up to prepare for school. Clutching her books to her chest like armor, Griffin slogged through the school. All over the hallways posters hung that read:

HELP RAISE PENNIES FOR THE PLANET!

Bring your donations to Science Night

Starring the band:

THE ALCHEMISTS

WE ROCK!

See Garrett Forester, Jason Scott,

or Griffin Penshine for early donations.

"WHAT!" Griffin couldn't believe it. Dashing down the hallway, she looked for Garrett.

Garrett turned around just as he was finished hanging another poster.

"Hey, Garrett," she said.

Garrett shrugged. "Hey."

"I'm really sorry," said Griffin.

"Apology accepted, because my band is gonna rock. I practiced all day yesterday. We're gonna be great. You'll see. I'm auditioning this Friday at the music center too. My mom called for me."

"Cool," said Griffin.

"I'm gonna be like U2 and Bono. They rock out and help the planet."

Griffin stared at him. "The posters are really nice."

"We need to make, like, twenty more. If kids come up to you, take their donations and save them in an envelope, okay? We'll add it all together later. Some of the guys from my band came over last night to help make posters. We should put a penny donation jug, like a Sparkletts container or something, in the front lobby to start collecting."

"Yeah, okay," said Griffin.

"Hi, Griff. Hi, Garrett," said Libby, waving as she came up to them in the hall. "Your posters are so cool! I can donate a ton of pennies for Pennies for the Planet. Griff, why didn't you call me back yesterday? My mom said I could have a sleepover on Saturday night for our friends. I would never, ever go to Samantha's party. Yuck! Mine will be a blast! We so won't look at skin products!" Libby giggled.

Garrett smiled.

Relief flooded through Griffin. Libby wasn't going to Samantha's party.

"I'm sorry, Libby. I wasn't feeling great last night."

"No worries. Text you later," she said, hurrying off to class.

"Griffin, I have an idea to make our booth totally awesome," said Garrett. "If we win, it's a five-hundred-dollar prize, you know. Can you meet Friday afternoon at the library?"

"Sure."

"Cool," he said.

"I'll see you there tomorrow, then," she said.

He turned the corner to put up some more posters.

Griffin's heart climbed up a notch. Pennies for the Planet was a great idea. If Garrett's band did practice, they had a shot at raising some money after all. Just then, Samantha, Martha, and Sasha slithered up to Griffin in the hallway.

"Hey, Griffin, are you meeting Garrett on *Friday night*? Is this a date? Is he your *boyfriend* or something?" taunted Samantha.

"No. He's not my boyfriend, Samantha," said Griffin. "We're doing our project together."

"Are you in the band? We saw your name on some of the posters," said Sasha.

"I'm collecting money," said Griffin.

"What? *Pennies?* That's not going to work!" The girls giggled. "Plus, we hear Garrett's band stinks!"

"Garrett's band doesn't stink, Samantha. They're amazing!" said Griffin, just as Garrett came up from behind them.

"It's all your fault we have to do this stupid project," said Samantha.

"It's not her fault," said Garrett. "All you have to do is find a cool topic."

"Puh-leez!" said Martha.

"Why are you guys so nasty?" asked Garrett.

Griffin had an urge to wish something nasty right back at the three girls with their spiteful, pinched faces. It took every ounce of her willpower not to.

"I'm not nasty, Garrett! I'm a model in my dad's commercials!" called Samantha, and the three girls huffed off.

* * *

True beauty is a light from within.

Chapter
30

✳ ✳
✳

I t seemed impossible that the town library could be so busy on a Friday afternoon. But with science night around the corner, most of Mr. Luckner's students were there working on their projects. Griffin, busy reading about alchemists at the study tables, was waiting for Garrett. After his music center audition he was supposed to meet her, and then her mom would drive them home. But it was hard for her to concentrate. Were the kids in the library mad at her? Did they think having to participate in science night was all her fault? Maggie, Madison, and Libby all had Mrs. Wilkens for science and didn't have to participate in science night.

Keeping her eyes and hands steady, Griffin continued to take notes about the alchemist Basil Valentine and his laboratory equipment: silver eggs, ancient shells, peacocks' tails, chunks of gold, and dragons' scales.

Eden Snyder, a classmate, came up to her table. "Hey, Griffin. Can I ask you something?"

"Yeah," she said.

"Do you know how to use the library's science database on this computer to find an old magazine article?"

Griffin knew this from her mom, who accessed the science database at home all the time.

"See, Eden, first you enter in . . ." Now three more kids gathered around her as she showed Eden.

"Hey, Griffin, did your mom ever say anything about black holes?" asked Robert Winbell.

"Yeah, they're collapsed stars. She says they're like a giant vacuum pit in space where everything gets sucked in. Even light can't escape. It gets suctioned down into the blackness."

"Cool. My partner and I gotta change topics."

"Would Griffin Penshine please come to the front desk? Would Griffin Penshine please come to the front library desk?" boomed the loudspeaker.

"Wait, Griffin!" called Caden Nosam, tapping on

Griffin's backpack. "Do you have any project ideas? My partner and I are switching topics too."

"You could research how to survive a bear attack. Some hikers who survived a bear attack said their backpacks saved them."

"Wow!" Caden said.

"I better go," said Griffin.

Eden, Robert, and Caden all thanked her. Griffin walked to the front desk toward the librarian. "Griffin, your mom is waiting outside," said the woman.

Griffin looked at her watch: five fifteen. Garrett hadn't shown up, and her mom had been waiting fifteen minutes for her. Walking to the car, she looked around for Stanley, the sad violinist.

"Stanley?" she called out. The sidewalk was desolate, filled with wet newspapers floating in puddles.

"Who's Stanley? Your *other* boyfriend?" Samantha snickered, heading into the library with Sasha.

"No one," said Griffin.

"You're friends with imaginary people?" Samantha said.

"You wouldn't understand," said Griffin.

"We don't want to!" they said, breaking into laughter.

Griffin gritted her teeth. *I wish . . . I wish . . .* She bit down hard on her lower lip. Desperately she wanted to wish something wicked on them. . . . *I wish . . .*

Don't stoop to their level, she heard her grandma's voice say in her head. *You are better than that.* Griffin took a deep breath. She hoped Stanley was okay.

Kristina carried a stack of books up the sidewalk toward the library. "Hey, Griffin!" said Kristina, stopping in front of her.

"Hi, Kristina," said Griffin.

"I'm really sorry I said that you and that penny were unlucky. I was really upset and didn't mean it. I finally convinced my mom to let me take ballet lessons, and my teacher thinks I have a lot of talent. I know it won't happen overnight, but who knows, maybe I can be an incredible dancer!"

"That's great," said Griffin. "I'm sorry I said what I did too. I didn't mean it either. I was really having a bad day."

They smiled at each other.

"Good luck on your project," called Kristina.

"You too," called Griffin, smiling. *Has the "most beautiful" wish been returned? Did something work after all?* she wondered.

Her mom honked.

Griffin got into the front car seat.

"Hi, Griff. Garrett's mom called and said she was sorry that Garrett's drum audition ran over so he couldn't get to the library. She asked if she could bring Garrett over to our house tonight so you two could work for a few hours instead. I invited her and Garrett over to dinner with us to celebrate."

"Celebrate what?" she asked. *That another wish just maybe was returned!* she thought.

"Garrett passed the drum audition! The drum teacher, Mr. Sanchez, was really impressed. He said Garrett has gobs of natural talent that needs to be tapped. He's going to take him on for free."

"That's awesome! What are we having for dinner?"

"A turkey."

"A turkey?"

"You've been talking an awful lot about wishes lately, so I decided to surprise you with a special dinner. I thought maybe you'd like a wishbone from a turkey."

Griffin stared at her mom. "A wishbone?" she said.

"Your very own. Well, to share with Garrett, too."

Griffin couldn't stop smiling.

* * *

Follow your bliss.
—Joseph Campbell

Chapter
31

※   ※
※

"Okay, are we ready?" asked Griffin's dad. Griffin's face glowed as she looked around the messy dinner table. Dinner had been delicious. Everyone had gobbled up the turkey, stuffing, and sweet potatoes. Griffin's mom presented the turkey's cleaned wishbone on a plate and brought it to the table.

"Here we are. The famous wishbone!" said her dad.

Garrett's mom laughed. "I used to do this as a kid. Haven't seen a wishbone in years!"

"Griffin, you grab one side of the wishbone," said her dad. "Garrett, you get the other one, and on the count of three, pull as hard as you can. One . . . two . . . three!"

Garrett stepped back, holding the larger piece of the wishbone over his head.

"Got it!" he shouted.

"Double congratulations today, Garrett! Since you pulled the larger piece of the wishbone, you get to make a wish," said Dr. Penshine.

"But it already came true," said Garrett, beating imaginary drumsticks in the air.

Everyone smiled.

"Well," said Griffin's dad, "if your first wish already came true, then you must be on a roll for a second one."

Griffin smiled. *If my own wishes can't come true, at least Garrett's can,* she thought.

Garrett made his second wish, but he wouldn't tell anyone what he had wished for.

"Hey, before you kids get to work, does anyone want a tour of my observatory? The sky is perfect for stargazing tonight," said Dr. Penshine.

Garrett, Griffin, Mrs. Forester, and Griffin's dad ventured up to the rooftop, with Griffin's mom leading the way. The night was cool and clear. "Let's see what's bright in the sky tonight. Well, we can all see the Little Dipper, or Ursa Minor, and look, there's the Pleiades rising in the East. Over there is one of my favorites: Cassiopeia."

"Cassio *what*?" asked Garrett.

"Here, Garrett, look through my telescope. Do you see those five stars?"

"Five stars in that giant zigzag in the sky?" he said.

"Yes, that's Cassiopeia. She was a beautiful yet wicked Greek queen. She claimed to be more beautiful than Poseidon's daughters. Poseidon, the king of the sea, was so offended that he sent a sea monster to destroy the city where she ruled. The only way to stop the monster was to sacrifice Cassiopeia's own daughter, Andromeda."

"What happened?" asked Garrett.

"Well, the brave hero, Perseus, discovered an ingenious way to kill the gigantic monster and rescue Andromeda. They lived happily ever after, and when they died, Andromeda and Perseus ended up as beautiful constellations."

"Cool," said Garrett.

Griffin smiled at her mom.

Until nine thirty that night Garrett and Griffin worked at the kitchen table, making clay models of the alchemists' tools and more posters for Garrett's band. With science night less than two weeks away, they were completely prepared. "I don't think I've ever finished a project early in my entire life!" said Garrett.

"Takes the pressure off," said Griffin.

"Yeah. Now I can jam with my band to get ready for the concert. Hey, could you give Kurt bass lessons? He really needs help. Come to our next rehearsal. I'll e-mail you the music."

"Sure," said Griffin. For a moment she longed to be in the band too, but she didn't dare wish that.

The doorbell rang. Mrs. Forester was back to pick up Garrett.

"Thanks for dinner. Bye, Griffin," said Garrett, smiling at her.

Griffin was glad it was dark, because for some reason she couldn't stop blushing. "Bye," she said.

"See you all soon at science night!" said Mrs. Forester.

"We look forward to it," said Griffin's mom.

Griffin ran to look at Andromeda and Perseus one more time.

✳ ✳ ✳

Shoot for the moon.
Even if you miss,
you'll land among the stars.
—Les Brown

Chapter
32

S aturday morning a gray sky domed over Dadesville. Griffin and Libby poured bright-colored paint into ice cube trays in Grandma Penshine's kitchen for their art lesson. Suddenly a cackling sound came from Grandma Penshine's living room. The noise did not sound like rain, or lightning, or anything natural. In fact, it sounded hideously unnatural.

"Did you hear that?" asked Libby.

"Yeah," whispered Griffin.

"Sounds exactly like —," said Libby.

"DON'T SAY IT!" said Griffin, jostling the tray of colors. They slopped all over her grandma's kitchen counter.

"Grandma? Is everything okay?" called Griffin. Her grandma was searching for some art books in the living room.

"Girls, you have to come see this," she answered.

Griffin and Libby ran to the living room. In front of the large bay window Grandma Penshine stood watching as three witches hobbled toward her front door carrying a sign that read, SHAKESPEARE IS NOT DEAD! COME SEE US AT THE TRAVELING GLOBE THEATRE CO. FESTIVAL.

"Freaky! It's like adult Halloween," said Libby.

"If that isn't impressive. Actors going door to door to promote their play. I really admire dedicated artists," said Grandma.

The doorbell rang.

"Grandma!" said Griffin. "Libby and I saw those actors in class already. Can we just not answer the door and do our lesson?"

"We can't dishearten other artists, even if they are in the dramatic arts," she said.

"Please, Grandma!" said Griffin.

"One minute only. I promise," said Grandma Penshine.

"Grandma, we really want to learn about . . . Who did you say we're learning about today . . . George?"

"Giorgione, the great Venetian painter from fifteenth-century Italy who changed the world with how he painted light and color—changed art forever, really. A true master."

The doorbell rang again.

"Let's just wish them well with their play," said Grandma. She opened the front door of her home, still in her art smock covered in shocks of color.

Griffin's head spun. The scent of spices, mandarin orange, dried lavender, cloves, and incense pounded in her head. She knew she had smelled that odor somewhere before.

"Hello," said Grandma Penshine. "What an inspiring sign you are all carrying."

"Thank you, my lady," cackled one of the witches.

"This is for you, my dame," said another. With her bony hand the hag passed her a brochure about the traveling festival.

"Shakespeare lives!" cackled the third witch.

"I couldn't agree more! The importance of keeping Shakespeare's great works alive is a responsibility of all artists," said Grandma Penshine. "Do you three know that my favorite line from Shakespeare is from *Hamlet*, act 1, scene 4: 'Angels and ministers of grace defend us!'"

Just then the sun burst through clouds, and glorious light beamed down. The three witches shielded their eyes, snatched back the brochure, and whirled their black shawls over their heads. Without a word they retreated down the walkway out into the street.

Griffin couldn't move. Her grandma and Libby watched until the witches had moved far down the road.

"Weird," said Libby.

"Those actors certainly are committed to their roles," said Grandma Penshine, shutting her door and locking it. "Can anyone believe this heavenly weather! The sky has shifted and is wild with joy!"

"Should we paint outside now?" asked Libby.

"On days like this the sky demands to be painted!" said Grandma, setting up an easel on the back porch. "If this were my last hour on earth, I could think of no better way to spend it than with you two wonderful girls, feeling the sun on my face, painting my flowers, and cherishing each and every whirl of color."

Tears sprung to Griffin's eyes. She watched as her grandma mixed paints as if mixing sacred medicine. She realized how much she'd miss her grandma if anything happened to her. Her voice always felt like a giant hug.

"We must paint the sun breaking through the cotton clouds just like Giorgione," said Grandma.

Griffin looked up at the sky and imagined she could jump into the clouds, float away on sunshine, forget witches, forget wishes, and forget all things gray and black.

"Grandma, were people nice to Giorgione?" asked Griffin.

"That's hard to say since he lived in the late 1400s, but I do know at first that people laughed at him. They said he didn't know the rules, his work was strange—too much color, too much magical light. Clouds were not *supposed* to be painted that way." Her grandma swirled some sapphire and crystal blues together on the canvas.

"Did he give up?" asked Libby.

"Certainly not!" she said. "How do you think I even know the name Giorgione more than five hundred years later? Personally, I think I know his secret."

"What?" asked Libby.

"I think he took some of those beautiful clouds he painted and stuffed them right into his ears. Then he couldn't listen to all the doubters who told him his stuff was too strange."

"Cool," said Libby.

"Griff, can you do me a favor?" called Grandma Penshine. "Could you please get my shawl in my bedroom? I just caught a chill."

"Sure," said Griffin, leaping up and going into her grandma's lavender bedroom. On the bureau, lilacs tucked in white porcelain vases swept perfumed shadows through the room. A blushing pink orchid rested languidly in a pot. The soft bed looked like a velvet pincushion. Grandma's shawl was flung over the rocking chair in the corner of her room. Suddenly Griffin noticed a wooden box inlaid with mother-of-pearl on her grandmother's dresser. Sticking out of the box was a skein of yarn. It looked exactly like the yarn in Mariah's box. Griffin froze.

White cotton curtains rustled in the breeze. Through the blinds, across the street, Griffin saw the witches holding hands in a circle.

"Griffin!" called Grandma Penshine. "Libby!"

Grabbing the shawl, Griffin dashed out of the room back to the kitchen patio. "Here, Grandma," she said.

"Girls, look!" said Grandma Penshine, pointing above her.

A dark cloud was marching head-on into the blue sky. "The sky is shifting! Right before our eyes. Quick!" Sinister, dark, heavy clouds were smothering the light. Libby and Griffin helped Grandma Penshine carry the canvases and tubes of paint inside. In one instant everything had shifted to gray. "Quick, girls! Please, shut my windows!" said Grandma. Griffin and Libby dashed through the house closing windows as rain pelted the house.

"What is with this weather?" said Grandma. "Downright

mystifying. One minute the most glorious sun, the next minute as gray as the storm's evil eye."

Lying in her bed Sunday night, Griffin thought about the phrase "as gray as the storm's evil eye." All weekend it rolled through her head. Even at Libby's superfun sleepover party the night before, she couldn't help thinking that those gray clouds had brought something strange to town. Something wicked. *Why did those actors come to my grandma's house?* In the rush of shutting all the windows, Griffin had forgotten to ask her grandma about the yarn. *Why does she have the same yarn as Mariah? The sky is shifting.* Griffin thought of Stanley. Was he out there in the rain with his violin? When would the witches leave town and go far, far away? Then she thought about Giorgione staring at the clouds five hundred years ago.

✳   ✳   ✳

Stuff your ears with clouds.

Chapter

33

Monday afternoon at school, Samantha and her friends had slipped notes into Griffin's locker. In Samantha's curly cursive writing the notes said: *Hi, Griff. I think I love you. From your new boyfriend, Garrett.*

Griffin stuffed these at the bottom of her backpack to dump into the garbage. Only one thing could make Griffin forget Samantha—a letter, which arrived in the mail after school. It was addressed to G. Penshine, and the return address read:

Mrs. Florence L. Daniellson Busby

c/o Sunflower Assisted Living Home

572 Myrtle Drive

Topeka, Kansas 66603

"Hi, Griff," called her mom from upstairs. She was decorating the nursery. "I'll be down in a minute. There's a letter for you on the table."

Griffin grabbed the letter and leapt up the stairs two at a time. After locking her door, she threw her backpack down and carefully opened the letter. Shaky words appeared on blue-lined notebook paper:

Dear G.,

I don't know who you are, but you must know me because I once threw a penny in the Topeka Inn fountain when I was an eleven-year-old girl. I held my penny so high and shouted with all my breath, "I wish for a puppy!" I still remember that summer day like it was yesterday, the warm Kansas sun on my face. It's funny, I can hardly remember what I ate for breakfast today, but I remember that day as clearly as

church bells chime on Easter Sunday. I never
did get a puppy. My little brother was allergic
to dogs, and then I married a wonderful man,
but he was allergic to dog hair too. I wonder
what in the world you could have of mine all
these years later? Please contact me at my
return address.

Sincerely,

Florence Lorraine Daniellson Busby

"Griffin?" called her mom through her bedroom door.
"I'll be right out," she answered.
"Who's the letter from?"

Griffin hesitated. She never lied to her mom, but she
couldn't risk having her hurt by Mariah's curse. Griffin
crossed her fingers and said, "An old lady. Part of a community service pen pal thing." She tucked the letter back into
the envelope and slid it under her bed before she opened her
door.

"I'm going to the store," said her mom. "Do you want to
come? I'm having serious pregnancy cravings for mustard,
orange juice, avocado, and barbeque potato chips!"

"Sounds really gross, Mom!" Griffin laughed.

"Doesn't it?" Her mom smiled and rubbed her big belly.

"I'm okay. I'm just gonna start my homework," said Griffin.

When Griffin heard the front door close behind her mother, she grabbed the phone and dialed information.

"City and state, please," said an operator.

"Topeka, Kansas. The Sunflower Assisted Living Home, please," said Griffin. She copied down the number and dialed.

"Hello, Sunflower. How may I help you?"

"Hello, my name is Griffin Penshine and uh . . . I'm a friend of Mrs. Florence Daniellson Busby. I'm thinking of getting her a top secret present, and I was wondering if your home allows pets."

"Yes, we do. Cats, small dogs, and certain kinds of birds are allowed. What kind of pet were you thinking of?"

"A small puppy."

"That sounds very nice."

"Thank you," said Griffin, and she hung up the phone.

"Griffin?" said her mom in her bedroom doorway.

"HUH!" Griffin jumped. She hadn't even heard her mom come in.

"What are you doing?" asked her mom with her hands on her hips.

"You're back already!" said Griffin.

"I forgot my wallet," said her mom. "Now, who in the world are you calling? Who is Mrs. Busby? What's this about a *puppy*?"

"Well, see . . ." Griffin just stopped. "Mom, before I tell you, I have two questions: How far is Dadesville to Topeka? And how much would a puppy cost?"

"It is a twenty-minute drive to Topeka from here, and a puppy rescued from the pound would probably be about seventy-five dollars."

"Mom, you know how you asked if I wanted a puppy a week ago?"

"Yes."

"Can I get one and then give it as a present to someone?"

"Griffin, *what is going on*?" said her mom.

She crossed her fingers behind her back again. "Mom, I was just trying to make an old lady's wish for a puppy come true. Kinda like a service project. Is that okay?" Griffin began to sweat.

"I need to think about this one. Let me talk it over with your dad," said her mother.

Griffin uncrossed her fingers.

At midnight Griffin jingled the last few pennies in her hand: "STOP," "popular," "world peace," and the unlabeled penny were still complete mysteries. Clasping two pennies in one hand and two pennies in the other, Griffin paced around her dark bedroom. *I've given away more than half the pennies, and I think a few wishes have come true,* she thought. The nightlight in her room cast strange shadows on the walls, mocking the faded stars on her ceiling. *I need to put new stars up,* Griffin thought. New sticker stars that glowed, shimmered, and shone to replace the dull ones. Her mom would help her with that; they'd probably replicate the real night sky. Griffin slowly parted her curtains, scanning the inky night roofs.

✳ ✳ ✳

Don't let your stars fade.

Chapter
34

✳ ✳
✳

I f this isn't a first!" called Dr. Penshine from the kitchen after school. "Mr. Castanara called from the music center and had to cancel your lesson. It seems he's caught a terrible cold."

"Really?" said Griffin. *My wish of becoming an amazing bass guitarist is definitely not coming true,* she thought.

"Since I thought you were going to be at your lesson, I made a doctor's appointment, and Dad won't be home until late tonight. Do you want to go over to Grandma's and hang out with her so you're not all alone in the house?" asked her mom.

"Sure," said Griffin. She wanted to ask her grandma about the yarn she'd seen in her box. After they played a few games of cards, she would ask her why it was just like Mariah's yarn.

Grandma Penshine was in her bed, covers tucked high all around her, when Griffin came over. "Hi, Grandma, how are you feeling?" asked Griffin. It didn't seem possible that her grandma could look so tired. What had happened to Giorgione and his soft clouds?

"Come here, my love." Grandma Penshine clasped her warm hands around Griffin's hand. "I've felt so tired the past few days. Like those dark clouds sapped some of my energy."

"Can I get you something, Grandma?"

"A glass of water, please. Oh, and in the kitchen on the table is a FedEx package that came for you today," said Grandma. "Why is it coming here for you, Griff?"

"I'll go get your water!" Griffin darted into the kitchen, where a thin FedEx envelope waited. Return address: Nome, Alaska. Griffin took a deep breath and pulled on the perforated cardboard strip.

Dear G. Penshine,

What do you have to tell me? I'm often on my boat, the Internet rarely works, and

mail takes forever here. Please use the
FedEx envelope and pre-addressed slip
I enclosed in this package. Just seal it
and drop the envelope in a FedEx bin.
Thank you.

Sincerely,

Brian Patterson Forester

Griffin's stomach tightened. *What* do *I have to tell Garrett's dad about him?* That Garrett used to wish for a dad, but he doesn't wish for such "stupid things" anymore? *What have I done?* She slammed the letter down, filled a tall glass of water, and trudged toward her grandma's room.

"Why such the long face?" asked her grandma, sitting up in bed.

"It's nothing, Grandma."

"Really? In my experience 'nothing' doesn't look like *that* on someone's face, especially not on yours. Do you want to tell me about that FedEx package? Did you open it?"

"Yes."

"And?"

"Well, see . . . Grandma, I'm not sure if I did something good or bad. I kinda wrote to someone and they wrote back," said Griffin.

"Maybe I can help?" said her grandma.

Griffin slumped on the side of her grandma's bed. "What if someone wished for something, and you wanted to help them get it. But then, when you thought about it, maybe they don't really want that wish to come true, and you've just made things worse for them."

"That's a tough one," said her grandma. "You know, that makes me think of a story. Can you see that bush outside my window?"

Griffin strained her neck to see out her grandma's bedroom window.

"The butterflies like it there because it's protected by the house, and the leaves give them lots of nourishing food to eat while they grow. Every spring I watch the butterflies struggle and struggle to break free from their caterpillar cocoons, and every spring I want to get my garden gloves and help them out of their cocoons, but that would be the wrong thing to do. Because if they don't do it themselves, they won't be strong butterflies. Actually, they might not even be able to fly if I help them. So, to answer your question, sometimes it's wrong to help people do things. They might not *want* help or even be *ready* for new things to happen. But there are always exceptions.

"One spring we had the oddest weather; one minute it was cool, the next minute hot as the desert, and this little half butterfly, half caterpillar didn't know whether to come out or stay in. Then he was almost gobbled up by a crow, so I shooed the bird away, picked up the cocoon, and nestled the little guy in the shoulder of a tree. So I did help him. I interfered right down to jingling bells at the crow. But when he finally broke free, he was one of the most beautiful butterflies I've ever set my eyes on. All summer he kept me company, fluttering his rainbow wings and visiting my windowsill. So sometimes it's best to leave things alone, and sometimes your heart tells you to jingle bells at the crows!"

"I'm not quite sure which one this is."

"When in doubt, trust your heart. How about we take a break and play a game of pistachio poker?"

They played eight games of pistachio poker until Grandma's eyelids flickered like two falling stars, and Griffin knew it was time for her nap. She realized she'd forgotten to ask her about the yarn. Carefully she gathered the deck of cards and placed them in a neat stack. Then she returned to the kitchen to read Mr. Forester's letter one more time.

✳ ✳ ✳

The heart has its reasons,
of which reason knows nothing.
—Blaise Pascal

Chapter
35

✳ ✳
✳

Midnight again, and Griffin fiddled at her desk, her eyes glued on Garrett's father's handwriting. Dark bags hung under her eyes from staying up so late the past few nights. Slowly Griffin began to write to Mr. Forester.

Dear Mr. Forester,

My name is Griffin Penshine and I'm twelve. Garrett and I are in the same science class in Dadesville, Kansas. I'm very sorry to have bothered you with a

Letter. Garrett and I were assigned by our science teacher to do a huge project together for science night. When my mom took us out to dinner after working on our project, Garrett told us he used to wish on his birthday for a dad. So I gave him a lucky penny and secretly wrote to you for extra luck to happen. I think he would be mad if he knew I wrote to you. I'm very sorry to have touched a cocoon I shouldn't have touched.

Sincerely,

Griffin Penshine

Griffin slid her letter inside the FedEx envelope and zipped it inside her backpack. The only FedEx drop she knew of was at the front office at school by Mrs. Davis's desk. During lunch tomorrow she would quietly place the envelope in the bin.

"Good morning, Miss Penshine," said Mrs. Davis from behind the desk in the front office.

"Hi, Mrs. Davis," said Griffin.

"What are you doing here? Certainly *you* can't be in trouble?"

"Can I put this in the FedEx bin?" she asked, holding the packet.

"Sure. They pick up at three o'clock. Whatcha dropping off?" she said.

"Just, uhh—a note," Griffin said.

Mrs. Davis swooped around her desk and peered into the FedEx bin. "'Brian Patterson Forester,'" she read aloud. "'Sender: G. Penshine.' Hmmm. Forester? I remember that name from entering school records. Is that Garrett Forester's dad?"

"Uhh, maybe. I'm just dropping something off for my grandma." *Brrringggg,* screeched the school bell.

"Oh, that wonderful lady I met the first day of school? Why is your grandma writing to Garrett's dad, sunshine? Are they acquainted?"

"It's about science night, that's all," said Griffin, through her clenched jaw.

"Look here! On the address line! Nome, Alaska! Garrett's dad lives in Nome, Alaska? Ain't that a hoot! Bear country! You know what they say about Nome, don't ya?"

Griffin shook her head, now dizzy, as the floor became quicksand sucking her down.

"They say," Mrs. Davis said, and started choking on her laughter, "there's no place like Nome!" Her laugh boomed all over the front office.

Griffin left the office and hoped Mrs. Davis wouldn't say anything.

* * *

To keep your secret is wisdom;
but to expect others to keep it is folly.
—Samuel Johnson

Chapter

36

S cience Night was only a week away, and Samantha and her friends were panicking, and panicking meant supervenom. It took every ounce of strength for Griffin not to wish wretched things on Samantha's clique. Like maybe Samantha's, Martha's, and Sasha's teeth would turn black and fall out, or they would all grow bushy beards. But darkness filling Griffin's soul in exchange for Samantha's sprouting a beard was not worth it. And some of the kids were excited about science for the first time. Audree constantly doodled blue-footed birds of the Galápagos. Photos of black holes plastered the inside of Robert Winbell's locker. Caden Nosam was bumping around the hallway with a stack of books, discussing bears with Mr. Luckner.

"Hey, Griffin," whispered Jason, a few desks down from her in social studies class. "Are you coming to band rehearsal today at Garrett's? Kurt really needs help."

"Yeah, I'll be there." For the past week she had learned all the songs for Garrett's band.

Trying to concentrate in class was becoming harder and harder for Griffin. Something was definitely wrong. The tingling-sinking feeling returned, and she'd had it ever since she'd left the front office.

A cold breeze swept through the hallway and throttled Griffin by the throat. As she unloaded books out of her locker, every hair on her neck shot straight up. She knew with one word what had happened.

"GRIFFIN!" yelled Garrett, rushing toward her, his face blistering red. "GRIFFIN," he said again, and now he was right in front of her. "DID YOU WRITE TO MY DAD?"

Her eyes grew large. "What?"

"I just bumped into Mrs. Davis, who said, 'Garrett, how neat that your dad lives in Alaska. There's no place like Nome!' I asked, 'How do you know that?'"

Griffin felt a steel rod zoom straight up her back.

"Mrs. Davis said, 'Well, your friend Griffin Penshine just sent him a letter.'"

"Can I talk to you after school?" she asked, looking down at her shoes as students passed by them in the hallway on the way to class.

"NO! I don't care if I'm late for class. I don't care if I never go to another class EVER!" Garrett was an erupting volcano.

Samantha and her group paraded by in a line, eyeing both Griffin and Garrett, who were standing, red-faced, inches apart from each other. "Look! Look! They're having a fight!" she heard the girls whisper as they passed them.

Griffin bit down hard on her lower lip and looked straight at Garrett. "Garrett," she said, and took a deep breath. "I'll tell you everything, but could we please talk after school?"

"NO! TELL ME RIGHT NOW!"

"Fine." The class bell rang, but Griffin didn't budge. "Garrett, you once said you wished for a dad. I wanted to help out your wish, so I Googled your dad and found out he lived in Nome. Then I asked him to please write me back.

I never thought anything would happen, *ever*. Then he sent me a FedEx package to put my next letter in. In my second letter I said I'm sorry, this is none of my business. I should not have written."

"I never want to see my dad! I hate you for writing to him! I'm not doing my science project with you, Griffin! I don't care if I fail! Do the stupid project yourself!" Garrett punched three lockers in a row and exploded out the school doors.

Griffin looked up from the swirling floor in time to see Samantha and her mean friends' faces pressed against the window of the classroom door, their shiny eyes like wolves'.

"Griffin Penshine! What are you doing out here? The class bell has already rung, and you're LATE!" shouted Mr. Blackwell, patrolling for tardy students.

"I—I—I was just getting my books," stammered Griffin.

"You're tardy. That means a thirty-minute detention after school in room 201."

"But, Mr. Blackwell   I . . .," pleaded Griffin, holding back tears.

She didn't hear anything for the last two periods of

school; only a giant blur and drone of buzzing surrounded her: "Did you and Garrett break up?" "Did Garrett dump you?"

Griffin knew she was lost inside one of Giorgione's inside-out clouds.

* * *

Ride out the storms when clouds hide the face of the sun in your life, remembering that even if you lose sight of the sun for a moment, the sun is still there.
—Blessing of the Apaches

Chapter

37

✳ ✳ ✳

Mrs. Forester called that evening, after Griffin had come home late from detention. From her bedroom Griffin could hear her mom talking. "We're so sorry, Mary Beth. So sorry. I know this must be very hard for Garrett and you. We can assure you Griffin had no idea what this meant to both of you. She was trying to be helpful."

Dr. Penshine clicked off the phone and knocked on Griffin's door. "Griffin, please open the door," said her mom.

But Griffin locked the door and buried herself under the blankets. She never wanted to go to school again. She never wanted to help another person again. She swore she would never write another letter or use another penny again in her whole life.

"Dad and I want to talk to you downstairs. Take fifteen minutes for yourself, but then we want you downstairs in Dad's office. No ifs, ands, or buts."

After Griffin heard her mom's footsteps go down the stairs, she took out Mariah's two boxes and put them on her bed. The "puppy," "STOP," "popular," "world peace," and the unlabeled penny remained. Griffin slowly took out Mariah's red ring, its huge garnet stone resembling trapped blood. Tears dribbling from her eyes, Griffin tried to see her reflection in the stone. But tonight there was no glow, just a dull red. One of Griffin's teardrops smacked the middle of Mariah's ring. Griffin brushed away the tear, leaving a smudge. Setting the ring back in the box, she scanned the remaining pennies. "Popular" looked dull and tarnished. Carefully she slid that penny out of the ring slit.

Long ago someone wished to be popular. Griffin wondered why that person had made that wish. Did he or she have that same suffocating feeling that Griffin did right now? Like the whole world was against her?

The grandfather clock chimed. Time to go downstairs and face her parents. The small desk light was glowing on her father's desk. Her parents sat on the couch together. Griffin slumped into the leather chair across from them.

"Griffin, it's time you told us what's going on," said her mom. "Garrett's mom is beside herself. She said Garrett is so upset. What made you write a letter like that?"

Griffin took a deep breath. She remembered what Mariah had said: *If you tell anyone about the curse, you are cursed for generations, and the person you tell will never have any of his or her wishes come true.*

Griffin chose her words carefully. "Remember when I met that lady, Mariah Weatherby Schmidt, at Mr. Schmidt's shop?"

Her mom nodded.

"She gave me a penny and a box of polishing cloths. But actually, in the box of cloths were some other lucky pennies. I was only trying to help make Garrett's wish for a dad come true. I gave him a lucky penny and wrote that letter to speed up his luck. Mariah also gave me a ring and a leather guest record book from the inn."

"May we see the ring and guest book Mariah gave you?" asked her dad.

"Okay." Griffin nodded and dashed upstairs to retrieve the box. When she returned, her mom examined the ring. "This stone is a garnet. It looks about six carats—worth quite a lot. They are never this large. The gold band is thick, too."

Together her parents opened the guest book and studied it, like careful archeologists. "An odd and interesting bequeathal," said her dad. "Reminds me of a quote from Ben Franklin. He said, 'If a man could have half of his wishes, he would double his troubles.'"

"I made a huge mistake. I just wanted to try to help Garrett."

"We know your intentions were good, but when you make a decision that affects someone else's privacy, you need to be respectful and really consider how the other person might feel."

Griffin nodded her head, as tears spilled from her eyes.

"I see here the name Florence L. Daniellson and the tiny word 'puppy.' Is this what the puppy thing is about?" said her mom. "This woman wished for a puppy?"

"I just thought it might be nice to make her wish come true."

"I see," said her mom.

"Garrett refuses to do the science project with me now. After all the work we did together, he'll totally get marked down if he's not there. He hates me too."

"First, I think you should write apology notes to Garrett and his mother. Try to explain what you meant to do."

"I told him already!" cried Griffin.

"Giving people time to calm down is best," said her mom. "Science night is still a week away. Maybe Garrett will change his mind. If not, you need to honor his choice, and we'll help you set up your booth. What do you want to do with Mariah's stuff?"

"Throw it in the garbage."

"Do you want to keep the ring?"

"No, it scares me," answered Griffin.

"I have an idea. Let's sell the ring, and any money you make we'll donate to Pennies for the Planet. I'll take care of it for you, okay?"

"Okay," said Griffin, tears still streaming down her face.

"Griffin," said her mom, "everybody makes mistakes or uses poor judgment once in a while, but it's what you do *next* that counts. Now, why don't you write those apology notes and get a good night's sleep."

Her mom stood up, kissed Griffin on the forehead, and went to make some tea. Her mom's warm kiss made her feel like crying even harder. Griffin turned to her dad. Between sniffles she said, "Dad, would you ever wish to be popular?"

"I'm sure a lot of people would like to be popular. It can make things easier or more pleasant, but popularity changes, grows, and can even get silly. The more honest and kind you are, the more the *right* kind of popularity comes to you."

"Yeah," said Griffin, wiping her wet eyes.

"Griffin, we love you—popular, unpopular, around the moon, and back again," said her dad.

Back in her bedroom Griffin dangled the "popular" penny in her hand and stood by her dark bedroom window. In the swirling moonlight she stared at the copper coin. Tomorrow she'd take the "popular" penny to school.

* * *

Popularity?
It is glory's small change.
—Victor Hugo

Chapter

38

✳　　✳
✳

D r. Penshine dropped Griffin off at school fifteen minutes early. In the lobby of the school well-lit display cases held trophies and notices for science night. In front of the cases was a water jug Garrett and Griffin had placed there for donated pennies.

The jug looked sad. Empty. Forgotten. Inside the jug two inches of pennies nestled at the bottom of the container, most of which Griffin and Garrett had donated themselves.

The halls were clear of kids, but a stampede of rushing students would burst through the doors in ten minutes. Griffin dug into her pocket and removed the "popular" penny. She wanted Pennies for the Planet to be the most popular charity, raising tons of money for the environment. Then, at least, this mess could count for something. Griffin was sure Garrett wished the same thing. But there was no way she could give it to him now. Griffin held the penny in her hand.

Samantha, Martha, and Sasha barged through the front doors of school. Huge designer bags were slung over their left shoulders, and they clutched chilled bottles of designer mineral water in their right hands.

Griffin's and Samantha's eyes locked.

Swiveling their heads, the girls looked at the pathetic almost-empty water jug. They laughed. "Checking on your project?" said Samantha. "We heard Garrett refuses to work with you. Too bad about *your grade*."

The penny started to burn into Griffin's palm. Round edges of copper pressed against her flesh, singeing her skin. Griffin took a deep breath. *Treat yourself with respect and ignore people who don't treat you with dignity* ran through her mind. The penny was scorching her palm, burning to be set free. Heat surged through Griffin's entire body. *Popular! Popular!* chanted through her head. Griffin fought to not throw the penny at Samantha's face. Her fingers could hardly contain the penny, now a hot coal.

"What's in your hand, Griffin? A frog?" said Samantha.

"Nothing," said Griffin.

"*Nothing* doesn't make your hand jump like that. Show us!"

"No," said Griffin.

"Show us!" said Samantha, moving closer.

"No, Samantha. You're such a bully," said Griffin, fighting to keep her hold on the burning penny. But it burned so badly that she lost her grip and the penny tumbled out along the cold floor.

Sasha ran for it, scooped it up, and placed it in Samantha's palm.

Griffin stood in front of her. Anger surged through her entire body.

"Look at this! This is too cute!" said Samantha, mocking. "A penny with 'popular' taped across it. Are you wishing to be popular? Do you carry around lucky pennies with labels on them for yourself?" The three girls howled with laughter.

Griffin bit her lip.

"You know what I think of you and your stupid penny?" said Samantha.

"I think this penny must be *nasty* being inside *your* pocket." She dumped some of her designer water on it, and the ink on the label began to bleed. The word "popular" spread in all directions.

Griffin glared.

"Oh, look at this, girls," said Samantha. "Her penny is ruined!" The girls laughed. "Maybe I should make a wish before it fades away . . ." In a baby voice, with her lips in a snarl, she mocked, "I wish Griffin becomes *superpopular*."

The three girls cracked up. Sasha laughed so hard she snorted. She added, "Don't forget her dork charity, too."

"And her dork charity, too."

"Here, Griffin, better take back your *lucky* penny!" said Samantha. But just as she threw it, the school bell blasted, and a charge of kids burst through the front doors along with a gust of wind. The penny flew through the air like a smoldering comet. In a ribbon of light the penny landed inside the water jug on top of the heap. The container lit up from within.

Samantha glared at Griffin. "Why did that penny light up? What kind of penny was that, anyway?"

"A lucky one," said Griffin.

※ ※ ※

All appears to change when we change.
—Henri Frédéric Amiel

Chapter

39

✴   ✴
✴

On science night, rubber sneakers squeaked over the gym floor that reeked of sweat and salt. Griffin had transformed the splatters and paint smudges Samantha's friends had squirted onto her sneakers by turning them into a cool design. She'd made the paint blobs look like a van Gogh–inspired rain forest.

While Dr. Penshine parked the car, Griffin dragged her bags through the gym in search of her booth. Passing Samantha's and Sasha's booth, number 23, Griffin locked eyes with Samantha. An electric sign over her booth blinked: THE SCIENCE AND JOY OF MY DAD'S DERMATOLOGY PRODUCTS. Samantha's father had donated the sign. When Griffin

219

looked closer, she noticed Samantha still had large warts all over her face.

"This lighting is unbearable!" screeched Mrs. Sloane. "Look at you! This is so bad for your father's business." Pulling more cover-up out of her purse, Mrs. Sloane slapped at Samantha's skin. The gold bracelets up and down Mrs. Sloane's arm jangled, calling even more attention to Samantha. "This is disgusting! I'm so embarrassed!"

Samantha glared at Griffin.

Griffin stared back. Mrs. Sloane made Samantha look kind. For the first time Griffin actually felt sorry for Samantha. Maybe there was a reason Samantha was so mean.

"Hi, Griffin!" said Audree, who was setting up her display table with facts about Darwin, the Galápagos Islands, and blue-footed birds.

"Wow, your booth looks great, Audree. Did you make that picture?"

"Yeah, my whole family. We spread out a giant sheet of paper on the living room floor and colored in the blue-footed birds. It really looks like a duck with powder blue feet."

"It's amazing. Good luck tonight," said Griffin.

"Thanks. You too. My mom said I worked so hard on this project that I can have a huge sleepover party! I'm calling everybody tomorrow!"

"Cool. Thanks," said Griffin, and she slid her heavy bags through the aisles, stopping at booth 17, which was assigned to Garrett and her. Doors opened to the public at six p.m., but Garrett was nowhere to be found.

Sighing, Griffin started to unpack all the things she and Garrett had made for their booth: poster boards, fact booklets, and clay models of alchemists' equipment. First she hung the huge poster board: THE ALCHEMISTS: GOLD, WISHES, AND FUTURE SCIENTISTS. She set up the models of the equipment the alchemists had used in hopes of turning ordinary metals into gold. Griffin put out a tray of gold sprinkled cookies she had baked with her mom.

"You doing okay, Griff?" asked Dr. Penshine, hauling more bags for the booth.

"Yup," she said.

"Looking really good!" said her mom. Carefully her mother took out a jar of pennies. Inside the jar, she and Griffin had displayed the "change the world" penny in a ring case. It was surrounded by a moat of pennies. Also displayed in the jar was a money order for eleven hundred dollars from the sale of Mariah's ring, made out to Pennies for the Planet.

Griffin smiled looking at this. When her mom had told her the ring was worth so much, Griffin had jumped up and down. She bet Mariah had never known her ring would one day help the environment.

Behind this jar Griffin and her mom tacked up poster boards that explained how pennies can be turned into gold, how when enough people give, each penny can help save the rain forest. *Saving the Amazon rain forest from being cut down is so important because trees supply most of the Earth's clear air and oxygen,* read her poster. Griffin had drawn the Earth with lungs in the middle and trees circling the planet.

Every time the gym doors opened, Griffin thought maybe Garrett had changed his mind and was showing up after all. Maybe he'd even forgive her.

"The booth looks great," said Mrs. Forester, walking over from the locker rooms.

"Mary Beth!" said Dr. Penshine.

"Nice to see you both," said Garrett's mom, smiling. "Hello, Griffin."

"Hi, Mrs. Forester." Griffin gulped.

"Thank you for your cards to me and Garrett. It meant a lot to both of us," said Mrs. Forester.

Griffin nodded. "Is Garrett coming tonight?"

"He's in the locker room practicing. The guys have been rehearsing night and day at my house. I was counting down to science night, just so I could get some sleep! I told him he has to come over to the booth and help as well. I don't want him marked down either, but he's being very stubborn."

"Okay," said Griffin with a sad smile.

Taking a deep breath, Mrs. Forester said, "I want you both to know something. Garrett doesn't know this yet. I plan to tell him at the end of science night. His dad flew into town late last night from Alaska. Ever since he received Griffin's letter, we've talked every day. He wanted to come support Garrett for science night. Maybe even stay awhile. I told him he can watch, but he should only talk to Garrett when the night is over so Garrett doesn't get nervous or upset."

Griffin froze. Garrett's dad was *here*? From Alaska?

"It's okay, Griffin," said Mrs. Forester, looking at her ashen face. "It might be very good for Garrett to have his dad around if we can all forgive one another. None of us ever stopped loving one another."

Griffin and her mom stared at each other. Then Dr. Penshine turned to Mrs. Forester and spoke. "Mary Beth, that sounds like big news. Congratulations."

"Thank you," she said. "I'd like you to meet Garrett's dad, Griffin. I want to show him the booth you both worked so hard on. One minute, okay?"

Griffin turned toward the back of the room. Sitting on the bleachers was a tall, handsome man with a brown beard.

Just like his picture, thought Griffin. Mrs. Forester waved him over, and he walked back to booth 17.

"Griffin?" he said in a deep voice.

"Hello," she said.

"Hi, I'm Garrett's dad," he said, and shook her hand. "I wanted to thank you for writing to me. I wouldn't want to miss this. I've missed so much already."

"I wasn't sure I should have written to you," whispered Griffin.

"I'm so glad you did. I hope one day Garrett is too. I'll be rooting for your booth and for The Alchemists tonight."

"Thank you," she said.

"You guys need any help?" he asked.

"I think things are under control, right, Griff?" said Dr. Penshine.

Griffin nodded.

✳ ✳ ✳

How does one become a butterfly?
You must want to fly so much that
you are willing to give up being a caterpillar.
—Trina Paulus

Chapter

40

✳   ✳

✳

Griffin! Griffin!" called Jason, out of breath and running toward her booth.

"Griffin, I have to talk to you!"

"What's the matter?"

"We need your help!" he said, panting. "Kurt got really sick, stage fright or something. He started to hyperventilate and then threw up everywhere! His mom's taking him home."

"Oh, no!" she said.

"We really want to play tonight. We've been practicing for hours every day. Do you think you could play his bass? We have all the music here."

Griffin looked at her mom.

"Up to you, Griff," said Dr. Penshine.

"We're on in twenty minutes!"

Griffin looked at the stage set up at the front of the gym. What if she couldn't play? *I wish to become an amazing bass guitarist. Did I return enough of the wishes so I'm not cursed with that wish too? Will I mess up onstage? Can I even do it?*

Slowly she turned to Jason. "You know, Garrett refused to do the booth with me tonight. If he'll come to our booth when the judges are here, then I'll play in your band."

"Awesome! I'll go tell him! Be right back!"

He darted away. "Twenty minutes?" said her mom. "Can you do it, Griff?"

"I know the music. I was supposed to teach Kurt, so I learned it."

"Go for it! I was in a band, you know," said her mom.

"You were?" said Griffin.

"Yeah. In college. The Rocket Girls."

They burst out laughing.

Jason came running back. "Garrett said okay. Come back to the locker room."

"Mom?" said Griffin.

"I'll watch the booth until you take over," she said.

Maneuvering through the booths about black holes,

electricity experiments, and jungle animals, Griffin located the locker room. Garrett stepped out from the door. Half his face was painted gold like a rock star.

"Hey," he said.

"Hey," said Griffin.

"Thanks for playing in the band," he said.

"Yeah," she said. "You'll come help with the booth when the judges arrive?"

"Yeah," he said.

They both smiled.

"We go up onstage in fifteen minutes. Here." He tossed her a tube.

"What's this?" said Griffin.

"Our costume," said Garrett. "We're The Alchemists, so you gotta paint half your face gold."

"Really?" she said.

The other three guys poked their heads out the door, one stacked on top of the other like circus clowns.

"Hey, Griffin. Thanks a lot!" they all said.

A big smile spread across her face. The boys looked so funny painted half gold—foolish, even. But Griffin shrugged and went to paint her face too. In the girls' locker room she stared at herself in the mirror. Her eyes glowed and her hair was shiny. Griffin peered into the mirror and thought about all those pennies, how she had tried so hard to give them back, break the curse, and help people. Griffin drew a long golden line down her face and painted the right side gold. On the left side of her face, around her three freckles, she drew shooting stars.

* * *

If you don't risk anything,
you risk everything.

Chapter

41

✳   ✳

✳

L adies and gentleman, your attention, please!"
called Principal Yeldah from the gym's stage. "We
are so proud to welcome you to science night!"

Clapping echoed through the gym and crackled through
the stage microphones. "Before the judges make their rounds
to evaluate each student's booth, Garrett Forester and his
band, The Alchemists, will be playing. They'll kick off our
evening to help raise money for Pennies for the Planet. This
fine charity helps turn pennies into gold for the environment. You all may notice there are five empty water jugs
in front of the stage. Please donate your change. Students,
dump out your mayonnaise jars of coins you brought from

home, and let's fill these containers! All proceeds go toward protecting our environment. Now, it is my great pleasure to introduce . . . The Alchemists!"

The lights dimmed except for a few spotlights hovering overhead. Applause inside the cavernous gym sounded like thunder. Griffin's heart was pounding louder than any drum she'd ever heard. *Why did I say yes?* she thought.

"One, two, three!" shouted Garrett, and the first song boomed through the speakers. Garrett's drums and Griffin's bass made up the rhythm section and set the base and anchor for the whole band. Kids cheered and started dancing. It was good the lights onstage were so bright and the audience so dark, because Griffin could hardly see anything. At first her fingers moved too slow. She messed up a few notes, but she recovered. Music and energy swirled around her. The Alchemists played three fabulous songs.

Out of the corner of her eye she saw what looked like shooting stars soaring in front of the stage. Turning her head, Griffin saw pennies being flung into the plastic containers. *Pings, plops,* and *whooshes* flew in electric zigzags as people threw money into the jugs. *Ping. Ping.* A dime bounced in too. *This is a different kind of ping!* thought Griffin. *Nothing stolen, just given. A silver raindrop. A shooting penny. A copper missile defending the rain forest.*

"Thank you! Thank you, everybody!" shouted Ethan and Garrett, both breathless as the lights flashed on. Roaring applause sounded like a jungle downpour through the gym. "Thank you. Please make your donations to Pennies for the Planet."

Mr. Reasoner and Principal Yeldah walked together onstage. "Folks," said the principal, taking the center microphone. "First, another big round of applause for The Alchemists!" Griffin could now see all the faces in the bright gym lights. Hundreds of faces! Libby, Audree, Maggie, Madison, the kids in her science class, and Garrett's mom all beaming with pride. Griffin's father was there holding her mother's hand, smiling at her. Everyone else was passionately clapping. Except Samantha. And Martha and Sasha. They just scowled. But no one noticed. In fact, everyone was having such a good time that no one paid much attention to them.

"We have a special announcement this evening. Tonight we will witness how small things can add up to very big things! Mr. Reasoner, " said Principal Yeldah, handing him the microphone.

Mr. Reasoner stood before the crowd. "Good evening, everyone. Tonight I would like to introduce one of my most dedicated metal shop workers, Alfred Coombs."

Griffin gasped. It was the silent boy from the back of the metal shop. Griffin held her breath.

"Alfred has been collecting pennies since he was five years old. One day in class, after Alfred heard about Griffin Penshine and Garrett Forester's fund-raiser idea, Alfred whispered a little something to me."

Alfred wheeled up on the stage two huge water jugs filled with glittering pennies packed to the top. "Each full jug of pennies is worth three hundred and fifty dollars. Alfred is donating two full containers to Pennies for the Planet!"

The audience erupted in applause. Griffin jumped up and down.

"That leaves the rest of the night to fill the five containers in front of the stage.

Also, Principal Yeldah informed me that we also have a donation from Nome, Alaska, for two hundred and fifty dollars."

Both Garrett and Griffin froze, looking out at the audience.

"Let's hear it for Alfred and for The Alchemists!" More clapping. Griffin looked at Alfred Coombs and smiled. He smiled his goofy grin back. He wasn't strange at all. He was fantastic.

"How about one more song from The Alchemists!" shouted Mr. Reasoner.

Thankfully they had one more song to play. It was called "Celebration."

✳   ✳   ✳

Never doubt that a small group of thoughtful,
committed citizens can change the world.
Indeed, it's the only thing that ever has.
—Margaret Mead

Chapter

42

✳ ✳

✳

When Griffin walked into science class the
next day, the entire school smelled like
warm chocolate chip cookies. The home
economics teacher and her students had baked cookies for
every student in the school to promote their department.

Griffin smiled, inhaling the scent that wafted in every
corner of the building. *I wish my new school smells like warm
chocolate chip cookies!* Maybe she was on track after all! She
hoped things had gone well for Garrett—meeting his dad last
night. She wondered if he'd even show up to school today,
with his dad in town. Maybe he would be mad at her until
the end of school, or even mad at her forever.

"Did you hear, Griffin?" asked Audree.

"Hear what?" asked Griffin, and she sat down in her seat.

"The newspaper is coming!" she said.

"What?" said Griffin.

"Shhhhh. Here comes Mr. Luckner," Audree whispered as the class bell rang. Just then Garrett darted in from the hallway and plunked into his seat.

"Well, class. I am humbled and amazed," said Mr. Luckner. "Your projects last night were out of this world. I'm so proud of all the hard work and *learning* that you've accomplished! Of course, the biggest winner of all last night was our own Earth. Now, Principal Yeldah has a special announcement."

BZZZZZZZZzzzz. The loudspeaker broadcast Principal Yeldah's voice through the school into each and every classroom. "Good morning, students. Congratulations on your stupendous work at science night. I'm so proud of all of you. A gigantic congratulations to last night's two team winners, Audree Stein and Aury Laww and Caden Nosam and Carol Peters. A huge thank you to both teams for their incredible generosity in donating their prize money to Pennies for the Planet. I need to say a special thanks to Griffin Penshine, Garrett Forester, Alfred Coombs, and The Alchemists for all their hard work protecting our Earth. In fact, in addition to Alfred's donation of two jugs of pennies, the remaining five jugs were filled last night, making the grand total for Pennies for the Planet five thousand fifty-three dollars and eleven cents!"

Applause erupted throughout the school. "Five thousand dollars!" kids shouted in classrooms. Griffin looked down at her desk and scribbled the math in her notebook:

- Seven jars of pennies (around $350.00 each) = $2,553.11
- An 1872 Indian Head penny (in a ring case) worth: $150.00
- Mariah's garnet and gold ring: $1,100.00
- An anonymous donation of $250.00 from Nome, Alaska
- Two $500.00 science night winner donations.
    TOTAL: $5,053.11 for Earth!

"Some of the most exciting news is that the *Kansas Tribune* called the school early this morning and wants to do a huge front page article about how young students can protect and help our planet. Next Saturday at eleven o'clock in front of the town hall Mayor Alexander will be giving an award to Griffin Penshine and Garrett Forester for starting the campaign. Television news channels are coming as well, and Dr. Fonda, a representative from Pennies for the Planet, is traveling from Washington, D.C., to accept a giant check representing the entire donation."

Applause exploded from the entire school, and Griffin and Garrett blushed simultaneously. When Griffin looked up, a note was on her desk.

Carefully, under her desk, she opened it:

Hey, great job last night. Amazing bass guitar.

I saw my dad last night. He's really cool. He's a champion fisherman. Sorry for the things I said.

G.

Griffin turned around in her seat.
Garrett smiled at her.

* * *

Help others achieve their dreams,
and you will achieve yours.
—Les Brown

Chapter

43

✳   ✳
✳

Mom?" called Griffin from her bedroom before school.

"Yes?" said her mom from the couch. Sweat beaded on her mother's forehead. Her breathing was heavy.

"Mom, are you okay?" asked Griffin, walking down a few steps.

"I'm fine. The baby is coming soon. I can feel it. Maybe she or he is coming early for your award! We are all so proud of you." She laughed and wiped her damp face with a cloth.

"You sure you're okay?" asked Griffin. All the wishes except four had been returned. Returning seven wishes had to count for something. "Puppy," "world peace," the unlabeled penny, and the "STOP" penny were left.

"Mom, before the ceremony next week, there's one more thing I have to do. Could we get a puppy for Florence Daniellson Busby, the lady who wished for one? When I called the assisted living home, they said pets are allowed there."

"Hmm," said her mom, and rubbed her belly. "I'll tell you what, let me make a few calls while you're at school. Can you give me the name of the assisted living home?"

"Sure."

When Griffin came home from school, her mom didn't move from the couch.

"Mom?" whispered Griffin. *I wish for a baby sister* sprang into Griffin's head. *Have I not tried hard enough? Will my mom and the baby be okay?*

"Griff," she said, waking up. "I have some good news." Her mom struggled to get off the couch. "I made a few calls, spoke to the Sunflower Home director, Mrs. Regan, and explained things. She was charmed by the puppy wish and said it's just what Florence needs. Dad can't drive you there on Saturday—he's got a morning appointment—and I think I should stick pretty close to home with the baby kicking so much. Garrett's dad agreed to take you and Garrett to pick out a puppy for Garrett and another one for Florence. I guess Garrett has been begging his mom for a dog for a year! I called ahead and paid for Florence's puppy, so you just choose one that would be best for an elderly lady, okay?"

"Thanks!" said Griffin, throwing her arms around her mom.

"It seems Mr. Forester is a big believer in wishes lately," said Dr. Penshine.

* * *

No dreamer is ever too small;
no dream is ever too big.

Chapter

A t exactly ten o'clock Saturday morning Garrett rang Griffin's doorbell. Griffin's heart raced. The sky had never been so clear, like a blue birthday streamer floating free above them.

"Hi, Garrett," said Griffin, opening the front door. She had checked her teeth three times for anything green. Libby had come over the night before and helped her pick out her outfit too.

"Hi," said Garrett. "Are you ready?"

"Yup," she said. *Did Garrett just blush? Could he be nervous too?* she thought.

Dr. Penshine called from the couch. "Have fun! I'm so proud of you both!"

Griffin slid into the backseat of the car.

"Good morning, Griffin," said Garrett's dad, smiling. They drove straight to the Dadesville Humane Society.

Puppies, cats, and rabbits were all up for adoption. Animals of all shapes and sizes were poking pink noses out of rows and rows of cages. Garrett bent down and looked into one. Tiny whimpers came from within. "Griffin, look!" There was a litter of five puppies bouncing around inside.

"Their mom got hit by a car, and they need good homes," said the volunteer.

"Look at that one!" said Garrett. One of the puppies was rolling over on her back, her tiny white paws wiggling in the air.

"Can I hold her?" asked Griffin. The volunteer placed the puppy in Griffin's arms. A pink tongue slurped all over her face. She giggled. Another one of the puppies was tugging hard on a piece of rope, wagging his tail.

"That's my dog!" said Garrett.

Garrett's dad bent down to look. "They both look great," he said.

At the front desk they filled out all the registration papers. Mr. Forester explained to the woman at the desk that they were taking Griffin's puppy straight to Florence; Garrett and his dad would come back for Garrett's puppy in the afternoon.

In the backseat of the car Mr. Forester carefully placed the puppy's cage between Garrett and Griffin so they could sit on either side of her. Her little paw kept shooting through the cage trying to touch them. Griffin giggled.

"What are you naming your puppy, Garrett?" asked Griffin.

"Nick, after Nicolas Flamel, or maybe Zosimos," said Garrett.

"Cool," said Griffin.

"How about you?" he asked.

"I think Florence should name her, you know?"

"Shhhhhh," Griffin said to the puppy as she bounced up and down in the parking lot of the assisted living home. "Don't ruin the surprise, silly!" Griffin dug her fingers in her pocket. The "puppy" penny was still there.

"Good morning. You must be Griffin and Garrett," said Director Regan, meeting them at the front door.

"Hi," they said in unison.

"I'm Garrett's dad, Brian Forester," he said. "The kids are so excited about this."

"We are too. Florence will be so happy. Who do we have here?"

The director bent down to pet the new puppy through the cage. "Girl or boy?"

"Girl," said Griffin.

"She's perfect. Right this way. I told Florence she had some visitors today. A certain G. Penshine who wrote her a letter and her friend Garrett Forester. Florence got all dressed up, even put rouge on her cheeks!"

Garrett's dad waited outside Florence's room with the puppy to keep her a surprise until just the right moment.

"Knock, knock," said the director, tapping on the door. "Florence, your visitors are here."

"Come in," said Florence.

Garrett and Griffin walked into her room. Florence looked very old and soft sitting in a chair by the window. She held out her hand to welcome them. "Welcome, welcome! Visitors to see me? What an exciting day. The real G. Penshine who wrote me a letter!"

Griffin said, "Nice to meet you, Mrs. Busby."

"Nice to meet you. Such a pretty and polite young lady. And who is this handsome young man?" said Florence.

"I'm Garrett," he said.

"What a beautiful couple," she said.

Griffin and Garrett both blushed a deep crimson.

"I don't get a lot of young visitors. I was so excited when I was told you were both coming to visit me today."

"Mrs. Busby, I was the one who wrote you that letter a few weeks ago."

"Yes, yes, if I recollect correctly, you said you had something of mine? What could you possibly have that might belong to an old lady like me?" she asked.

"Someone gave me something that once belonged to you," said Griffin, reaching into her pocket and pulling out the penny. Gently she placed it in Florence's tender hand.

"A penny?" said Florence, and she studied it.

"I met a very, very old lady before she died," said Griffin. "She said she overheard you make a wish for a puppy. She wrote down the wish in a guest book next to your name. She labeled your penny: 'puppy.'"

"NO!" gasped Florence. She held the penny tight in her hand and closed her eyes. "I remember that summer day clearly, that scorching Kansas sun on my cheeks. I threw that penny high into the air. With all my heart I called out, 'I wish for a puppy!'"

A long sad pause penetrated the room. "My very own

penny *returned*. My very own wish taken out of the fountain and returned to me after all these years. What a beautiful thing to make something right even after so many years have passed." From her faded-blue eyes a single tear tumbled onto the penny.

A glow crescendoed through the entire room as if the sun had charged on full blast and poured the brightest rays into Florence's room. "Well, that's not all," said Garrett. "Dad!"

Mr. Forester walked into the room holding the puppy. "Good morning, Mrs. Busby. I'm Garrett's dad. The kids have brought you a present. A surprise just for you!"

Mrs. Busby's eyes lit up like a child's. Jumping up from her seat, her arms flew into the air, springing the penny like metallic confetti. "A puppy! A puppy!" she shouted, clapping her hands together.

"Do you want to hold her? She's a gift for you," said Griffin.

"A puppy for me?" She cried even harder now, her shiny eyes crinkling. "A puppy to keep me company! It's hard to feel lonely with a bouncing pup! My first puppy in my whole life!" She held out her old hands to the dog. Florence giggled like a girl as the puppy licked her wrinkled cheek. Laughter and tears came at the same time. "What's the puppy's name?"

"It's up to you," said Griffin.

"Penny! That's her name!" said Florence. "This is a wish worth waiting for!"

* * *

Never give up on a dream just because it takes time.
The time will pass anyway.

Chapter

45

✴ ✴ ✴

Griffin waved as Garrett and his dad backed out of her driveway. Griffin couldn't wait to call Libby and tell her everything! Garrett was so nice and cute and kind to Florence and funny and smart and great at drums. Also seeing Florence so happy made this one of the best Saturdays that Griffin had ever had. Smiling and giddy, Griffin couldn't wait to tell her mom about the puppy, too. She pushed on the front door, but it was locked.

"Mom, I'm home!" she called. She rang the front doorbell. But no one came. Three times she rang the bell. "Mom! Dad! Hello!"

Nothing.

Griffin checked her cell phone. She had turned it off at the Sunflower Home. Her message box was full. "Griff, it's Dad. Everything is okay. I'm taking Mom to the hospital because the baby is on the way! Hang tight. When you get this message, please go to Mrs. Jasper's house. I called her, and she is going to stay with you until I can come pick you up. I love you."

"Griffin!" called Mrs. Jasper, running toward her. "I've been looking out my window for you ever since your dad called me!"

"Did the baby come yet?" asked Griffin.

"I don't know. I just know your mom is in the hospital, and your grandma, too."

"Grandma, too?" Griffin's heart started racing. "They're both at the hospital?"

"Yes," she answered.

Griffin trembled. *This is my fault,* she thought. She still had three pennies. Although she had given away "no homework," "most beautiful," "change the world," "a dad," "baby," "success," "popular," and "puppy," the "STOP" penny, "world peace" penny, and the unlabeled penny remained in Mariah's black box.

"Your dad said it would be best if you stayed with me until he calls, and then I can drive you to the hospital to be with him. Okay?" she said.

"Okay," said Griffin slowly, finding it hard to breath. "Both Mom and Grandma in the hospital," she whispered to herself. *Why is my grandma there? Will the baby be okay?*

They walked over to Mrs. Jasper's house. Eight times Griffin called her dad on his cell phone, but he did not pick up.

Griffin sat at Mrs. Jasper's table, pushing noodles around on her plate. When the phone finally rang, it sounded like a fire alarm and a rushing ambulance to her ears. Mrs. Jasper grabbed for the phone. "Hello. Yes, she's fine. We're eating some dinner. Is everything okay?" There was a long pause and Griffin gripped the sides of her chair. "Here's Griffin!"

"Hi, Griff," said her father, sounding exhausted.

"Hi, Dad."

"You doing okay?" he asked.

"Yeah," she said. "Are Mom and Grandma okay?"

"Your mom is doing just fine. I'm so sorry you had to come home to a locked house. My cell phone ran out of battery in the hospital and I was with your mom in the delivery room. But . . . dun, dun, dun . . . drumroll, please. . . . You have a new happy, healthy baby brother!

A baby brother! The opposite of what I wished for! thought Griffin. *A healthy baby brother is fine with me!*

"Caelum came a week early. We were worried he might be born in the car! We almost changed his name to CAR-lum!"

Griffin laughed so hard tears filled her eyes. "Caelum's here! I have a brother!"

"Yes, a healthy, happy baby brother. Ten pounds! As big as a turkey! A giant baby! He and Mom are doing great."

"Can I come see him?"

"Yes. Mrs. Jasper is going to bring you to the hospital."

"And Grandma?" she asked.

"Grandma had a fall this morning. Hit her head on the floor, Griff," said her dad softly.

"Is she okay?" asked Griffin, her stomach squeezing up into her throat.

"She goes in and out of sleep, in and out of making sense."

"Can I see her?" asked Griffin, starting to shake.

"Yes, we'll see her together, okay? Hang tight, kiddo. I love you."

"I love you, too, Dad." Griffin sat down and couldn't stop crying. *Grandma*.

* * *

Don't let the teardrops rust your shining heart.
—Holly Cole Trio

Chapter
46

✳ ✳
✳

D ad!" called Griffin, running to her father in the hospital corridor, hugging him close. With a crumpled shirt and matted hair, he looked like he hadn't slept in a week. "Are you okay?"

"I'm great. Do you want to see your new baby brother?"

"Dad, is Grandma okay too?" she asked.

"She's sleeping right now. We'll go see her after you meet your brother, okay?"

"Okay," she said.

Together they walked down the long antiseptic-smelling corridor. "This is it. The east wing. New arrivals!" he said. "Room 302." She walked faster and faster. Poking her head inside the room, Griffin gazed at her mom sleeping with a bundle in a crib next to her.

"Mom!" said Griffin.

"Griff," said her mom, lifting her head from the pillow, smiling. "Come here," she said, reaching out her hand.

"Are you okay?"

"Couldn't be happier! It seems Caelum was ready to come into the world, *immediately*!" She laughed and kissed Griffin on the forehead, smoothing back her hair.

"Can I look at him?" she asked.

"Of course," said her mom.

Leaning over the plastic box next to her mother's bed, Griffin whispered, "Hi, Caelum." She touched his tiny pink hand, five velvet fingers. "He's so soft!"

"Like when you were born," said her mom.

"Really?"

"Really," said her mom, smiling and leaning back against the pillows.

"Do you need anything?" asked Griffin's dad, holding his wife's hand.

"Just rest," she said.

"Of course," he said, kissing her. "Griff, let's let Mom sleep a little. It's not every day your mom gives birth to a ten-pound baby almost in the middle of Main Street!"

Dr. Penshine giggled.

"Let's see Grandma and then have some dessert together in the cafeteria. Then we'll come back, say goodnight again to mom, and go home, okay?"

"How long will Mom and Caelum be in the hospital?" she asked.

"Two nights," said her dad. "Standard procedure."

"And Grandma?" asked Griffin.

"I don't know," said her dad.

"Oh," said Griffin, holding back tears.

He put his arm around her as they tiptoed away from Dr. Penshine and Caelum, who were now both sound asleep.

✳ ✳ ✳

A good parent is the greatest treasure.

Chapter 47

✳   ✳
✳

W here's Grandma's room?" asked Griffin.

"On the eighth floor," said her father.

"The doctor made an exception to let you see her in intensive care when I told him how close you two are."

They rode the elevator to the eighth floor and walked to room 807. Unlike her mom's room, this room was very dark. Grandma Penshine was not propped up in bed, but looked shrunken under the white sheets. Up and down went her chest, IVs taped to her arms. Griffin shuffled to the side of the bed.

"Grandma?" Griffin whispered, taking her grandma's soft hand in hers. "We love you."

Suddenly Griffin felt her grandma's palm press inside hers. A nurse talked quietly with her dad in the doorway. "Griff, I want to look at Grandma's X-rays with the doctor. Stay with her, okay? I'll be right back." He left the room.

"Grandma," Griffin whispered, "did you see the sky today?"

"Yes," she whispered. "I still see it."

"Yes!" said Griffin, squeezing her grandma's hand harder.

"It was perfect blue, like satin streamers," breathed Grandma Penshine, and slowly her soft brown eyes opened.

Griffin hugged her.

A peaceful smile spread over Grandma Penshine's face, and she looked at Griffin. "Come closer," she whispered.

Griffin bent her head down so she was cheek to cheek with her grandma.

"In my bedroom," her grandma said, and took a deep breath, "there is a box on my bureau. Look inside it."

"What's in it?" asked Griffin.

"You look and see. I love you," she said, her chest heaving another breath.

"Grandma?" said Griffin.

She squeezed Griffin's hand.

"Will you get well?" asked Griffin. She tried not to cry,

but her tears started falling, like raindrops dotting her grandma's sheets.

"I am well, Griff. Just old. Half as old as a Galápagos turtle," she said, taking a deep breath. "My bones are getting fragile, but I can't complain. They've done such a good job all these years. Plus, it's almost time to see your grandpa and all our flowers again. I've been having the most beautiful dreams about two white doves; at night they land on my windowsill, singing so sweetly. Don't you waste one wish for me to get well when my heart feels so good. It's your turn to make wishes for yourself. I already made all my wishes, and they all came true. I love you forever, my wish giver." She closed her eyes and fell asleep.

* * *

Go confidently in the direction of your dreams!
Live the life you imagined.

Henry David Thoreau

Chapter

48

✳   ✳

✳

Dr. Penshine and Caelum came home from the hospital on Monday, but Grandma Penshine was still in intensive care. *Why did Grandma call me a wish giver? Why did she want me to look in the box on her bureau?* thought Griffin as she folded baby clothes in Caelum's nursery. Griffin's mom placed the "baby" penny in a silver baby cup that had once belonged to Griffin's dad. "A lucky penny! What a nice way to start life, don't you think?" said her mom, bending over Caelum cooing in his crib.

"Yes," said Griffin, inhaling the sweet scents of the nursery. Everything smelled like baby powder, lotion, and new things. Griffin's parents let her take the day off from school to welcome Caelum and her mom home. In the afternoon she'd visit Grandma Penshine at the hospital.

"Griff, could you help Dad pack some of Grandma's things to take to her at the hospital? She really wants her favorite socks and a deck of cards," said her mom.

"Sure," she said.

Griffin's dad grabbed a duffel bag before driving to Grandma Penshine's house. Griffin could not wait to look in the box on her grandma's bureau.

Carrying a bag, Griffin went with her dad down the hall into her grandmother's bedroom. The floor creaked. Griffin turned on the lamp in the bedroom, illuminating the flowered wall-paper and cozy blankets on the bed. She wanted nothing more than to curl up next to her grandma and play pistachio poker. But the bed was empty. Inside the room, while her father packed some things, Griffin spied the inlaid mother-of-pearl-box on top of the bureau. She picked up the box and brought it to her grandma's bed. Slowly she opened the box. Inside were four things: a blue sapphire ring, the skein of old yarn, a large flat white stone, and one supershiny Indian Head penny.

Griffin heart raced. The ring looked identical to Mariah's ring except that the stone was blue. The yarn was exactly like

Mariah's gray spool. The smooth white stone was the same shape and size as Mariah's black stone mirror.

"What do you have there?" asked her dad.

"Nothing," she said, and gulped.

"Can you help me over here?"

"Yeah. Dad, I want to bring Grandma's favorite box to the hospital to show her, okay?"

"Okay," said her dad. "We'll drive straight there."

In the car Griffin kept the box sealed closed on her lap. *Why does Grandma Penshine have the same yarn as Mariah? Why does she have a ring just like Mariah's, except it's blue? Why does she have a stone just like Mariah's except it's white? Why did she save one supershiny penny?* The penny was as bright as the first one Mariah had given her.

Once they arrived at the hospital, Griffin and her dad took the elevator to intensive care. Griffin hurried in front of her father, clutching the box, until she reached room 807. Griffin stopped dead inside the room. It was empty. She gasped, and tears welled in her eyes. The hospital bed was perfectly made with an ugly mustard-colored blanket tucked tightly between the white sheets. The room had a plastic sterile smell. Griffin didn't move. Her father came in behind her. "Huh?" he said.

"Dad?" whispered Griffin. Chills shot up her spine.

"Maybe they've moved her. Surely we would have been called if anything had happened."

Just then a nurse bumped into them. "Mr. Penshine?"

"Yes. My mother was here in room 807."

"We just moved her to the second floor. She's doing so much better. She woke up, talked a bit, nibbled some toast, even told a joke."

"Good news," said her dad with a deep sigh.

Griffin reached for her dad's hand.

"What room is she in?" asked Mr. Penshine.

"Follow me. She now has a full river view. The staff here call the rooms on this side of the hospital the riviera!" said the nurse. They followed her to the other side of the building. "I'll go get her doctor for you folks."

In her new room Grandma's chest billowed up and down. She dozed in a deep slumber. Griffin's dad bent over and kissed her on the cheek.

Relief flooded through Griffin as she ran to her grandma's bedside.

"I need to go talk to the doctor. You stay here with Grandma."

Griffin took her grandma's hand. "They put you in the riviera rooms," she said. "They knew you'd want to hear the river."

Griffin walked to the window and slid it open. A light breeze blew through the room, and Grandma whispered from her bed, "Griff."

"Grandma!" She ran to her side again. "Are you okay?"

Grandma Penshine did not raise her head from the pillow, but she smiled. Her cheeks had a healthy pink glow for the first time since she'd been taken to the hospital. "Sky is bright blue, isn't it?" she said. "The breeze always feels different when it's clear."

"Yes, it's blue. Grandma, I brought your box for you."

Grandma Penshine smiled and propped herself up a bit in bed. She looked like a flower, soft and delicate. She took Griffin's hand. "I have something to tell you."

Griffin nodded, standing by the bed holding Grandma Penshine's hand. "On Saturday morning your parents told me you were bringing an old lady a puppy, fulfilling a wish for her." She adjusted two hospital pillows behind her lower back. "They told me about that woman Mariah Weatherby Schmidt, who had given you a box of these so-called lucky pennies. I have something very strange to tell you." Then Grandma Penshine leaned forward, looking straight into Griffin's eyes, and whispered: "I met her once when I was a girl."

Griffin stared. Her mouth hung open.

"'That's the only time my life ever crossed paths with Mariah, but it was enough."

"You met Mariah!" gasped Griffin.

"Right before my daddy and mama bought their farm, we were traveling through Kansas and stopped at an inn at the crossroads of Topeka."

"The same inn!"

"That inn was a sparkling oasis with a beautiful fountain bubbling in the scorching Kansas heat. I begged my daddy for a coin to throw in the water to make a wish. I must have been around eleven years old. I had the most glorious red hair, like you do now."

Griffin stared at her grandma's thick white hair.

"I wasn't born with white hair, you know," she said, laughing. Grandma Penshine sat straight up in bed now. "We only stayed one night at the inn, and it was some of the hottest weather I have felt in all my life. I kept hearing these plunks and pings coming from the courtyard."

Griffin thought, *Of course my grandma heard plunks and pings!*

"I looked out my window, and people were throwing coins in the fountain wishing for things: bicycles, money, blocks of ice, wheat to grow. I smiled, hoping those people's wishes all came true."

Griffin stared at her grandma with huge eyes.

"But then late that night, when it was still so hot and I could hardly sleep, I looked out my window and saw the young lady from the front desk, Mariah Weatherby Schmidt, swooping up coins in the blue moonlight. I hid in the darkness and watched. Every wild knot in my stomach signaled that *I was witnessing a real live Wish Stealer*!"

"What did you do?"

"The next morning when we were leaving the inn, I begged my daddy for *three coins*. He said, 'Didn't I give you a coin yesterday?' I told him, 'Yes, sir. But I was only practicing then. Today is something different.' He gave me *three new coins* and said, 'Make your wishes, but don't forget—the *real luck* is inside you.' But you see, I knew what I had to do. On that hot Kansas morning, I held my *first penny* high in the sky. Right before I threw it into the fountain, I yelled at the top of my lungs 'STOP!' I think everyone in the whole inn could hear me! I only meant for Mariah to hear. I wished for her to stop stealing people's wishes."

Griffin gasped.

"I saw Mariah rustle the curtains in the office window. Her dark silhouette stood behind the white cotton." Grandma Penshine was getting excited, remembering what she had done. She threw off the hospital sheets and leaned forward. "The *second penny* wish I did not say out loud. Silently I wished and tossed my coin high like a leaping ballerina. It hit the water, making a million sparks." Grandma Penshine clapped her hands and looked up as if she could see the shooting sparkles.

"What was your second wish, Grandma?" whispered Griffin, tensing her whole body. She remembered what Mariah had written in her letter. *The penny I gave you at the shop flew like a leaping ballerina vaulting into the water. That person didn't say her wish out loud, but her penny was as dazzling as her long red hair.*

"What was it? What was your second wish, Grandma!" said Griffin, her heartbeat going mad.

"For lost wishes everywhere to be returned," she said, smiling.

Griffin clutched the side of the hospital bed.

"The *third penny* that my father gave me I put deep inside my pocket to keep. I decided then and there that I was going to make my own luck in this life. That's what the penny in my old box is for, to remind me that we all make our own luck and to keep my dreams and wishes safe."

"Then you don't believe in luck or curses?" asked Griffin.

"I only believe in love, hard work, and a little bit of magic." A beautiful smile lit up Grandma Penshine's face.

Griffin grabbed her grandma's box on the side table and opened it. She held that old penny in her hand. It bounced.

Griffin broke into a magnificent smile. When she caught her breath, she explained to her grandma what Mariah had said about the unlabeled penny. The unlabeled penny was indeed Grandma Penshine's second wish, made when she was a little girl with hair the color of autumn leaves, caramel kisses, and blazing sunsets.

"I hadn't thought about Mariah for ages, but it all made sense. Mariah stole my 'STOP' stealing penny. What a journey for that penny to land with you!" Reaching out both her arms, Grandma Penshine said, "Griffin, I think you've become the best thing any human can ever be. You're a brave, brave wish giver. I love you."

✳ ✳ ✳

What lies behind us, and what lies before us,
are tiny matters compared to what lies within us.
—Ralph Waldo Emerson

✳ 266 ✳

Chapter

49

✳ ✴ ✳

"Grandma, I have the three last stolen wishes here in my pocket." Griffin reached into her pocket and read the labels. "'STOP,' the unlabeled penny, and 'world peace.' What should I do with them?"

"'World peace' is a mighty big one, but not impossible. That one is for you to decide, but 'STOP' and my unlabeled penny have been returned to me, thanks to you, Griffin!"

Griffin smiled. She had returned three pennies to their original owners. Griffin placed the unlabeled penny and "STOP" in Grandma Penshine's hands. At that exact moment the river sounded loud and clear in both their ears. Grandma Penshine winked. She got out of bed and walked over to the window with the river below. Slowly she closed her fingers around her two returned pennies and made the exact same wishes. Then she pitched the two pennies into the river.

Plunk! Plunk! rippled and rang out.

"Such a beautiful sound!" said Grandma Penshine.

Griffin's dad walked back into the room. "Mom, you're up!" He hugged her. "You look as healthy as a young girl!"

"I feel like a young girl when I'm with Griffin," said Grandma. "Griffin, can you please bring me my box?"

Griffin placed the mother-of-pearl box on her grandma's lap. Carefully her grandma opened it and removed the large sapphire ring.

"What's the ring for? Mariah had one just like this, but it was red."

"Your grandfather gave this to me long, long ago. He bought it in the fanciest jewelry shop in Topeka. If I recall correctly, I remember him saying it was a very old sapphire, an antique from England. It was once part of a large garnet and sapphire ring. But the jeweler separated the two stones, made them into two different rings. Grandpa bought the blue stone instead of the red one. Blue is the color of the sky and ocean, two things that will always help you remember joy. The ring is now a gift for you."

Griffin slipped the ring onto every finger. It fit best on her thumb.

"We should probably save the ring until you grow up," said her dad.

"Yeah," said Griffin, smiling. She stared at the ring. It looked like a piece of the sky set still and clear behind glass. *Could Mariah's ring once have been attached to my grandma's ring? Mariah and my grandma entwined?*

"And the yarn? What's that for?" Griffin held up the yarn by one end as if it were a dead opossum's tail.

"I bought that yarn more than seventy years ago!"

No wonder it smells so bad! thought Griffin.

"That yarn is from a carnival that passed through Topeka. The man selling it said it was magic yarn. Said the skein of yarn was the thread of life, and if you saved it and didn't cut it, you would live a long, long life. All I know is that he sold it for way more than regular yarn ever cost! Oh, and the yarn salesman was very handsome!"

"You fell for that?" teased Griffin's dad.

"It was worth every penny. Even back then I liked the idea of a long thread of life—made me happy just thinking about it. I think every young girl in Topeka that summer bought some of the magic yarn!"

"Is it magic, then?" said Griffin.

"It must have been magic to the man who sold it for more than plain old yarn is worth!" said her dad, laughing.

"Can I have it?" asked Griffin.

"It's yours," said Grandma Penshine.

Even though it was musty, Griffin planned to keep it in her Mysterium Collection Box.

"What is the white stone for?" asked Griffin.

"I found it by the river bank when I was a girl. I thought it looked so polished and pretty, like a giant pearl. Must have been washed by the water for at least a hundred years to be so smooth. I never found a use for it, but always thought I would one day."

"Can I give it to Charlemagne?" asked Griffin. "I've been looking for something special for his terrarium for the longest time."

"What a great idea! I bet it was once a throne for a turtle king. He'll love it!"

Griffin smiled. Then suddenly a shadow crossed her face. "Grandma, Mariah gave me a black polished stone, said it was a mirror to see the future, but it scared me and I broke it by accident."

"That's a lucky accident. Don't go looking into objects to tell yourself the future, look only in your heart. What did you do with all the black broken pieces?" she said.

"I forgot to clean them up. They're under my bed."

"If you don't mind, I'd love to have them to use to pot my orchids," said Grandma Penshine. "Orchids are some of the most lovely, graceful flowers in all of nature, but the funny thing is they bloom best in tiny jagged rocks and coarse bark. Somehow they can use ugly things to create incredible beauty."

"I'll sweep the pieces up for you," said Griffin, smiling. She thought of all the pink, orange, and yellow orchids that filled her grandma's house. "What will you do with your last lucky penny, the one you always kept in your box?"

"That is also for you. I made many wishes on that penny long ago, and they all came true."

"They did?" said Griffin.

"Yup. You know what was the best wish of all?" said her grandma.

"What?" said Griffin and her father at the same time. Griffin smiled.

"A long, healthy life full of love," said Grandma Penshine. "If you've got that, you've got everything."

✳ ✳ ✳

The best wish of all.

Chapter

50

The sounds of drums, horns, trumpets, and whistles
electrified the air. A marching band, reporters,
and news cameras gathered in the sunshine
in front of the town hall. Dr. Fonda, the representative for
Pennies for the Planet, had traveled to Dadesville to collect
the check the bank had written after counting all the coins.

Griffin, Garrett, and Alfred had been invited to stand
on the platform set up in front of the town hall next to the
bubbling town fountain, where in half an hour they would
present the giant check to Pennies for the Planet. Mayor
Alexander of Dadesville would speak first and introduce them.
Thousands of people packed onto the town green. Hot dog

vendors, potters, artists, and local clubs all set up booths.

Griffin was supposed to meet Garrett by the information booth at ten thirty a.m.

"Griffin!" called Garrett.

"Hi," she said, smiling. She carried a bag of *Go Green, Save the Earth*, and *Peace* rubber wristbands in a bag to hand out to kids.

"Hi. This is pretty cool," said Garrett, looking around at the huge crowd gathered to celebrate something they had started. Griffin gave him a Save the Earth band. They wove their way through the booths.

"Griff!" called Libby, running up to her and hugging her. Maggie, Madison, Audree, and a few other girls were right behind Libby. "This is so awesome. Congratulations!"

"Thanks," said Griffin. She hugged her friends, each wearing a different wristband. Everywhere people munched on organic popcorn and licked raspberry clouds of cotton candy. People kept stopping to congratulate her and Garrett as they made their way to the stage. Garrett stopped to talk to some of his friends.

Passing Mr. Luckner, Griffin saw him eating a huge cotton candy cone like a little kid. "Hi, Mr. Luckner," she said.

"Hi, Griffin. I'm thinking I should assign a big science project every year!"

"Maybe," said Griffin, still smiling. She gave him a *Go Green* wristband.

Mrs. Gideon came up to Griffin. She wore a colorful velvet patchwork skirt and a necklace of small clay squares with Chinese symbols for good luck on each one. "I'm so proud of you! I hand-copied one of Shakespeare's sonnets for you as a gift for all your work to help our planet. It's Sonnet XCIV. The one we talked about in class."

Griffin accepted the beautiful poem written in calligraphy. When she read it, the lines that meant the most to her were: *"They that have power to hurt and will do none . . . and to temptation slow . . . They are the lords and owners of their faces."*

"Thank you so much, Mrs. Gideon. I will save this forever," said Griffin. She gave her a *Save the Earth* wristband and rolled the poem into a scroll to keep in her Mysterium Collection Box. With Mariah's curse she could have hurt a lot of people, and she had been tempted. But she'd refused to end up a rotted lily with cruelty twisted in her face. She now knew: She owned the light inside her.

"Griffin," said Mrs. Gideon, "the Traveling Globe Theatre Company left town early. Some kind of date mix-up. Such a shame. I'd hoped our class would get to see them perform."

"We could always do *Hamlet* and act out some scenes. My grandma taught me the best line from that play. 'Angels and ministers of grace defend us always against curses, evil wishes, and witches!' Or something like that," she said, smiling.

"*Hamlet?* What a wonderful idea! Maybe we will! I could still use my Festering Lily Perfume too," she said, and winked.

"It's your perfume?" said Griffin.

"I bought it at a Shakespeare festival at Stratford-upon-Avon in England. I thought it would be perfect for a lesson on sonnets!"

Griffin laughed. So that was Mrs. Gideon's secret!

Samantha, Martha, and Sasha—overdressed with giant bags with nothing inside them, and high-heel shoes that kept sinking into the mud—stood a few feet in front of her. No one noticed them. People were more interested in celebrating saving the planet and listening to the music than talking about Samantha's new clothes. Samantha called to her, "Griffin, what are you handing out?"

Griffin said, "Wristbands to remind people about what's important. Do you three want one?"

"Okay," said the girls.

To Martha, Griffin gave a *Go Green* band; to Sasha, *Save the Earth*; and to Samantha, *Peace*.

The three girls studied the bracelets like they were reading a foreign language.

"Uh, thanks," said Samantha and her gang, trying on the bracelets.

"They look good on all of you," said Griffin, and she kept walking.

Garrett called out, "Griffin, over here!" He waited for her at the platform base. Mayor Alexander was ready to go up and speak. Principal Yeldah was one step behind him.

Griffin waved and ran toward Garrett.

"Look!" gasped Griffin as she approached the stage. "Look! It's Stanley! And Aurora!"

"Who?" said Garrett, looking up at the two musicians onstage ready to play.

"Stanley from the library and Aurora the harpist from the music center. Aurora!" called Griffin. "Stanley!"

They both waved. Stanley, smiling, came to the edge of the steps to greet them.

"Hello!" he said, bending down to talk to them. "Thanks to you and that lucky penny, my life has done a flip-flop."

"Really?" said Griffin.

"That old penny you gave me was magic! While I was walking down the street, I accidently dropped it. The penny rolled away, and I thought, 'Just like my life, things rolling away.' But for some reason I chased that penny, and when

I scooped it up, I stood face-to-face with a poster on a telephone pole. It was a picture of Aurora playing in town! Well, I scrounged some money to buy a ticket to her concert, and on the way out I bumped into her. I gave her my CD, and the rest is history!"

Aurora came to the edge of the platform. "Hello, Griffin and Garrett. Congratulations."

"Thank you," said Griffin.

"Thank *you* for helping me find Stanley. Talent like his doesn't come along very often. When I listened to his CD, I knew he was the accompanist I needed! I invited him to come on tour with me."

"Cool!" said Garrett.

Griffin beamed.

"Attention, please. Your attention, please!" said Principal Yeldah through the microphone.

"We're really proud of you both!" said Aurora.

The surging crowd shifted their attention to the stage. Griffin's heart pounded. From the raised steps she observed people pushing closer to the platform. Garrett's dad and mom held hands in the crowd close to the stage. Libby cheered nonstop.

Griffin's head spun when she noticed the top of a Sunflower Assisted Living Home van. Painted on the van's windows in bubble letters were the words "Thanks, Griffin! Thanks, Garrett! Yay, Penny!" Had Florence and her friends come to the ceremony?

Griffin's heart hammered harder.

"Are you ready?" whispered Principal Yeldah from the stage.

"Yep," said Garrett and Griffin. Alfred from the metal shop arrived on the platform steps.

"Hi, Alfred," she whispered.

"Hi," he whispered back, and blushed. Griffin guessed he was nervous too.

"Ladies and gentlemen," said the principal, "may I have your attention please on this beautiful Saturday in Dadesville!"

Everybody cheered.

"Today we celebrate the remarkable efforts of some of our young citizens who want to make a difference in our world, want to make changes and help our planet. By starting small but thinking big they raised awareness and collected pennies for the charity Pennies for the Planet. From the incredible support of fellow students and the town community, more than five thousand dollars was raised for our planet! I am also thrilled to announce that the Bank of Dadesville has matched that sum, making the grand total for Pennies for the Planet ten thousand dollars!"

Wild applause erupted from the audience.

Griffin, Garrett, and Alfred all high-fived.

"Here today is Dr. Fonda to accept a check that will be used to prevent deforestation of our Earth. But before we present the check, would Griffin Penshine, Garrett Forester, and Alfred Coombs come up onstage and share a few words?"

Alfred spoke first. "Hi, I'm Alfred Coombs, and my grandpa always told me two things: He said, in the words of Benjamin Franklin, 'A penny saved is a penny earned.' I've been saving pennies all my life. But the second thing my grandpa always said to me was, 'Never be penny wise and pound foolish,' which means know what's really valuable and don't skimp on the important things! I'm so proud to give all these years of saved pennies to help our planet."

Applause again rang through the audience.

Garrett took the microphone and spoke next. "I'm Garrett Forester. Doing your part for the planet is cool! Helping out is like being an alchemist—you can turn regular old things like pennies into gold! Peace out!"

Cheers rolled in giant waves across the town green.

Griffin unfolded her speech and scanned the sea of faces. Her mom, her dad, and Caelum were smiling like bright stars in the crowd.

"Good morning, everyone. My name is Griffin Penshine, and I would like to thank all the students of GWL and the citizens of Dadesville for everything you have done to help support our Earth by donating to Pennies for the Planet. It is so important to donate, but it is also important to do little things that add up to big things, like planting a tree every year, not littering, or taking the time to campaign against something you believe is hurting our environment. A lot of little efforts can add up to giant efforts.

"If you look very, very closely at a penny, in supersmall letters you'll see a phrase on each and every one. It reads *e pluribus unum,* which means 'out of many, one.' Just think, if *many* small groups all over the *whole world* did their part—and we combined all those caring groups into *one group*—think how much we could accomplish to stop the destruction of the rain forest! To stop pollution! To promote peace!

"Out of all the pennies that were donated, I have one very old penny that I have been saving for a long time." Digging into her pocket, Griffin pulled out the "world peace" penny. "Some people believe that if you wish on a penny, your wish just might come true if you don't let anybody say, 'It's impossible! Give up! Don't be silly!' Never let Wish Stealers steal your dreams and make you ashamed for trying. I was hoping all of you out there today could make a wish for world peace on this penny."

The townspeople roared applause in response.

Griffin counted, "One! Two! Three!"

The audience hushed, and everyone made a silent wish for world peace.

Holding the penny high over her head, Griffin tossed the penny into the town fountain. It arced in the sky, sparkling like the most brilliant beacon.

✳ ✳ ✳

You must be the change
you wish to see in the world.
—Gandhi

Acknowledgments

Thank you to the Wish Givers in my life who helped make this book possible. A profound thanks to my editors: Ellen Krieger for her extraordinary notes, and to Fiona Simpson for her astute guidance. A heartfelt thanks to my manager, Fonda Snyder, whose intelligence and warmth make working with her a joy and honor. An incredible thank-you and love to my husband, Alexander Trivas, and to Hadley. Thank-you to my mother for her optimism, and to my father for his quiet and deep love of art. A huge cheer for my brothers, Scott and Todd. A very special thanks to my in-laws, Sam and Stephanie.

To the great teachers of my life: Dr. Anderson, Mrs. Burns, Mrs. Skripol, and Professor Gelfant, I am grateful. Thank-you to the sparkly-eyed librarians: Mrs. Fournier, who let me hide out at recess in my elementary school library to read; and Linda Clancy, my hometown librarian who saved the *Anne of Green Gables* books for me. Thank-you to the excellent team at Simon & Schuster, especially Bess Braswell, Paul Crichton, Andrea Kempfer, Alyson Heller, Bernadette Cruz, and Venessa Williams. To the friends who offered support, insights, or expert information during the writing of *The Wish Stealers*, I am grateful: Aury, Lauren, Robert, Heather, Scott, Jyoti, Regan, Jake, Jennie, Todd, Elaine, Sarah, Jonathan, Stephanie, Benny, Ilana, Sara, Dennis, McCabe's Guitar Store, Dr. Thomas, Griffin, Audree, Lily, Gabrielle, Yapha,

Elisabeth, Jared, Michelle, Maria, Crystal, Nicole, Madison, Bob, Maggie, Ketaki, Eileen, Eden, and Merly.

To the readers of this book, I wish you so much good luck, love, and happiness as you navigate the Wish Stealers of the world, keep company with the hearty Wish Givers you encounter, and pursue, protect, and believe in your wishes.

Check out

PENNIES FOR THE PLANET

to see how you can make a change!

www.penniesfortheplanet.org

* * *

Check out

THE WORLD WISH PROJECT

Creative wishes for positive change.

www.worldwishproject.com

Check out

www.tracytrivas.com